THE GLASS
MAGICIAN

ALSO BY CHARLIE N. HOLMBERG

The Paper Magician

THE GLASS
MAGICIAN

CHARLIE N. HOLMBERG

47N⬤RTH

Text copyright © 2014 Charlie N. Holmberg
All rights reserved.

Published by 47North, Seattle

www.apub.com

Amazon, the Amazon logo, and 47North are trademarks of Amazon.com, Inc., or its affiliates.

ISBN-13: 9781477825945
ISBN-10: 1477825940

Cover design by becker&mayer! LLC

Library of Congress Control Number: 2014940615

Printed in the United States of America

Dedicated to my sister Alex, who believed in me before anyone else did.

CHAPTER 1

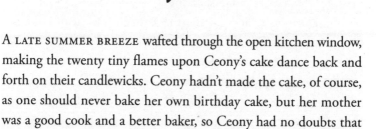

A LATE SUMMER BREEZE wafted through the open kitchen window, making the twenty tiny flames upon Ceony's cake dance back and forth on their candlewicks. Ceony hadn't made the cake, of course, as one should never bake her own birthday cake, but her mother was a good cook and a better baker, so Ceony had no doubts that the confection, complete with pink cherry frosting and jelly filling, would be delicious.

But as her parents and three siblings sang her birthday wishes, Ceony's mind wandered from the dessert and the celebration at hand. Her thoughts narrowed in on an image she had seen in a fortuity box just three months ago, after reading Magician Emery Thane's fortune. A flowery hill at sunset, the smell of clover, and Emery sitting beside her, his green eyes bright, as two children played beside them.

Three months had passed, and the vision had not come to fruition. Ceony certainly couldn't expect otherwise, especially since children were involved, but she ached for a wisp of the thing. She and Emery—Mg. Thane, that is—had grown close during her appointment as his apprentice and the subsequent rescuing of his heart. Still, she longed for them to be closer.

She debated her birthday wish and wondered if it would be better to ask for love or for patience.

"The wax is dripping on the cake!" Zina, Ceony's younger sister by two and a half years, exclaimed from the other end of the table. She tapped her foot on the ground and blew a short lock of dark hair from her face.

Margo, the youngest sister at age eleven, nudged Ceony in the hip. "Make a wish!"

Taking a deep breath and clinging to the crisp memory of the flowery hill and sunset, Ceony bent over and blew out the candles, careful not to let her braid catch fire.

Nineteen went out, casting the kitchen into near darkness. Ceony quickly huffed and extinguished the twentieth rogue candle, praying it wouldn't count against her.

The family applauded while Zina rushed to turn on the one electric bulb that hung from the kitchen ceiling. It flickered thrice before popping, sending a downpour of glass and darkness onto the partygoers.

"Well, great," complained thirteen-year-old Marshall, Ceony's only brother. She heard his hands slide around the table, searching for matches—or perhaps sneaking an early taste of cake.

"Watch your step!" Ceony's mother cried.

"I've got it, I've got it," Ceony's father said, shuffling toward the cupboard-shaped shadows. A few moments later he lit a thick candle, then fished around in a drawer for an extra bulb. "They really are handy, when they work."

"Well," Ceony's mother said, ensuring none of the glass had landed on the cake, "a little darkness never hurt anyone. Let's cut the cake! Do chew with care, Margo."

"Finally," Zina sighed.

"Thank you," Ceony said as her mother expertly sliced a triangle of birthday cake and handed it to her. "I really appreciate this."

"We can always spare a cake for you, no matter how old you get," her mother said, almost chiding. "Especially for a magician's apprentice." She beamed with pride.

"Did you make me something?" Marshall asked, eyeing the pockets of Ceony's red apprentice apron. "You promised you would two letters ago, remember?"

Ceony nodded. She took a bite of cake before setting the plate down and retreating into the tiny living room, where her purse hung from a rusted hook on the wall. Marshall followed excitedly, with Margo at his heels.

From the purse Ceony pulled out a flat, Folded piece of violet paper, feeling the slight, familiar tingling of it beneath her fingers. Marshall looked on as she pressed it against the wall and made the last few Folds that formed the bat's wings and ears, careful to align the edges of the paper so the magic would take. Then, holding the bat's belly in her hand, she commanded it, "Breathe."

The paper bat hunched and pushed itself up on her palm with the small paper hooks on its wings.

"Amazing!" Marshall exclaimed, seizing the bat before it could fly away.

"Careful with it!" Ceony called as he rushed toward the back hallway, to the room he, Zina, and Margo shared.

Reaching into her pack again, Ceony pulled out a simple bookmark, long and pointed at one end. She handed it to Zina.

Her sister crooked an eyebrow. "Uh, what is this?"

"A bookmark," Ceony explained. "Just tell it the title of the book you're reading and leave it on the nightstand. It will keep track of what page you're on by itself." She pointed to the center of the bookmark, where she'd overlaid a small square of paper. "The page number will appear here, in my handwriting. It should work for your sketchbooks, too."

Zina snorted. "Weird. Thanks."

Margo clasped her hands under her chin. "And me?"

Ceony smiled and rubbed Margo's orange hair, a color that matched her own. From the side pocket of her bag she pulled a small paper tulip. Green paper comprised its stem, and red and yellow paper formed its six petals, which overlapped at the edges and alternated in color.

Margo's mouth formed a perfect *O* as Ceony handed her the flower.

"Set it in your window, and in the morning it will bloom, just like a real flower," Ceony said. "But don't water it!"

Margo nodded excitedly and followed Marshall's path back to the bedroom, cradling the tulip as though it had been crafted of glass.

Ceony sat in the living room to finish her cake with her parents while Marshall and Margo played with their new spells in their room. Zina had headed to Parliament Square for a date. Bizzy, the Jack Russell terrier Ceony had been forced to leave behind upon accepting her apprenticeship, curled up lazily at Ceony's feet, lifting her head every now and then to beg for a crumb.

"Well," Ceony's mother said after her second piece of cake, "it does sound like it's going well for you. Magician Thane seems like a very nice teacher."

"He is," Ceony said, hoping the poor lighting masked the blush creeping up her cheeks. She set her plate on the floor for Bizzy to lick. "He's very nice."

Ceony's father clapped his hands down on his knees and let out a long breath. "Well, we'd better get you a buggy so you can head back before it's too late." He glanced out the window at the night sky. Then he stood, opening his arms for an embrace.

Ceony jumped up and hugged her father tightly, then her mother. "I'll visit soon," she promised. Without traffic, it took just over an hour to get from Emery's cottage to Whitechapel's Mill Squats, so Ceony didn't drop in as often as she would have liked. She felt certain she could make the trip in a quarter hour on Emery's paper glider, but he insisted that the world wasn't ready for such eccentricity.

Ceony's father called the buggy service, for which Ceony insisted on paying, and soon Ceony sat in the back of an automobile, chugging past the tightly spaced flats of the Mill Squats on a cobbled road winding between town houses. She passed the post office, the grocer, and the turn for the children's park, taking the meandering route out of the quieting city. Soon her buggy's lights were the only ones on the road. Ceony stared out the open window at the stars, which grew in number the closer she drew to Emery's cottage. Invisible crickets sang from the tall grasses that lined the road out of London, and the river running alongside it bubbled and churned.

Ceony's heart beat a little faster when the buggy pulled to a stop. After paying, she disembarked and stepped past the cottage's menacing spells, which disguised it as a run-down mansion with broken windows and falling shingles. Beyond the fence, the home stood three stories high, made of soft yellow brick and surrounded by a garden of vibrant paper flowers, buds closed for the night. A light burned in the library window. Emery had been away all week at a Magic Materials in Architecture conference, which the Magicians' Cabinet had insisted he attend. Ceony quickly straightened her skirt and rebraided her hair to smooth any loose ends.

The padding of paper paws capered behind the door before Ceony could finish turning her key. Once inside, Fennel jumped into her arms and wagged his paper tail, barking his whispery bark. His dry paper tongue licked the base of Ceony's chin.

Ceony laughed. "I wasn't even gone a full day, silly thing," she said, scratching behind the dog's paper ears before setting him back down. Fennel ran in two short circles before jumping onto a pile of paper bones at the end of the hallway. When enchanted, those bones formed the body of Emery's skeletal butler, Jonto, to whom Ceony had finally become accustomed. Still, being routinely awoken by a paper skeleton dusting her headboard had been enough motivation for Ceony to start locking her door.

"Be gentle," Ceony warned Fennel, who had taken to chewing on Jonto's femur. Fortunately, his paper teeth did little damage to the bone. She stepped past the mess and flipped on the light in the kitchen. The simple room had a small stove to her right and a horse-shoe of cupboards to her left, behind which rested the back door and the icebox. She didn't see any dirty dishes in the sink. Had Emery eaten?

Ceony thought of preparing something just in case, but a flash of color from the dining room caught the corner of her eye.

There, on the table, sat a wooden vase full of red paper roses, so intricately Folded they looked real. Ceony approached them slowly and reached out a hand to touch their delicate petals, which had been Folded of the thinnest paper Emery had in stock. The flowers even had complex, fernlike leaves and a few rounded thorns.

Beside the vase rested an oval hair barrette made of paper beads and tightly wound spirals, heavily coated with a hard gloss to keep it from bending. Ceony picked up the barrette and thumbed its ornamentation. It would take her hours to craft something this intricate, let alone the roses.

The roses. Ceony pulled a small square of paper from the center of the bouquet. It read "Happy Birthday" in Emery's perfect cursive script.

Her stomach fluttered.

Ceony fastened the barrette behind her ear and slid the note into a side pocket of her purse, where it wouldn't wrinkle. She took the stairs to the second floor, pinching her cheeks and adjusting and tucking her blouse as she climbed. The electric light from the library drew a lopsided rectangle on the hardwood flooring of the hallway.

Emery sat at the table on the far side of the book-lined room, his back to Ceony. He leaned on one hand, fingers entangled with the dark, wavy locks of his hair. His other hand turned the page of an especially old-looking book, though Ceony couldn't tell which one. A long, sage-green coat hung over the back of his chair. Emery owned a long coat in every color of the rainbow, and he wore them even in the middle of summer, save for July 24, when he had thrown the indigo coat out the window and spent the rest of the day Folding and cutting a blizzard's worth of snowflakes. Ceony still found the snow-flakes every now and then, wedged between the icebox and the counter or collected in crumpled piles beneath Fennel's dog bed.

She knocked the knuckle of her right index finger against the doorframe. Emery started and turned around. Had he really not heard her come in?

He looked tired—he must have been traveling all day to be home by now—but his green eyes still burned with light. "You're a sight for sore eyes. I've done nothing but sit in hard chairs and talk to stuffy Englishmen all week." He frowned. "I also believe I've become something of a food snob, thanks to you."

Ceony smiled and found herself wishing she hadn't pinched her cheeks so adamantly. She turned her head to showcase the barrette. "What do you think?"

Emery's expression softened. "I think it's lovely. I did a good job on that."

Ceony rolled her eyes. "How modest. But thank you, for this. And the flowers."

Emery nodded. "But I'm afraid you're now a week behind in your studies."

"You told me I was two months ahead!" Ceony frowned.

"A week behind," he repeated, as though not hearing her. And perhaps he didn't. Emery Thane had a talent for selective hearing, she'd learned. "I've determined it's best for you to study the roots of Folding."

"Trees?" she asked, thumbing her barrette.

"More or less," Emery replied. "There's a paper mill a ways east of here, in Dartford. They even have a division for magic materials, not that it matters. Patrice requested your attendance for a tour of sorts, the day after tomorrow."

Ceony nodded. She *had* gotten a telegram from Mg. Aviosky about that.

"We'll start there. It's quite exciting." Emery chuckled.

Ceony sighed. That meant it wouldn't be, but she wasn't surprised. How exciting could a paper mill possibly be?

"We'll take a buggy at eight that morning," the paper magician continued, "so you'll have to rise early. I can have Jonto—"

"No, no, I'll be up," Ceony insisted. She turned back for the hallway, but paused. "Did you eat? I don't mind cooking something if you're hungry."

Emery smiled at her, the expression more in his eyes than his lips. She loved it when he smiled like that.

"I'm fine," he said, "but thank you. Sleep well, Ceony."

"You, too. Don't stay up too late," she said.

Emery turned back to his book. Ceony let her gaze linger on him for a second longer, then went to get ready for bed.

She set the roses on her nightstand before falling asleep.

CHAPTER 2

AFTER FRYING SOME CREPES with strawberries and cream for breakfast, Ceony returned upstairs and opened her bedroom door and window to keep the space from getting too hot. She played fetch with Fennel using a balled stocking for a few minutes, then returned to the spell Emery had assigned her before he left for the conference—a paper doll of herself.

The paper doll had proved tricky, not because of the abstract concept, but because the initial step required the assistance of another person. Ceony couldn't very well trace her own silhouette onto paper, after all. With Emery gone and Jonto unable to hold a pencil steady, Ceony had telegrammed Mg. Aviosky to request the assistance of her apprentice, Delilah Berget. Delilah, a year Ceony's senior, had taken two years to graduate from Tagis Praff instead of Ceony's one, so they'd overlapped. Since Mg. Aviosky kept Delilah frightfully busy, the tracing hadn't commenced until the evening before Ceony's birthday.

Now Ceony sat on her bedroom floor with a pair of scissors she had purchased from a Smelter two years ago. The twin blades could cut through anything, and would never dull. Ceony studied them for a moment before taking them to the long sheet of paper etched with her front-facing silhouette. Had she become the Smelter she'd once dreamed of being, she would likely know how the spell worked by now. Not that she regretted the decision to apprentice under Emery, whether or not it had been hers to make.

Cutting out the silhouette was a slow process; Emery had warned her that one wrong cut would ruin the spell, and she didn't want to start over again. Ceony had managed to cut out the left foot and up to the left knee before Emery appeared in the doorway, his indigo coat sweeping about his calves.

Ceony carefully pulled back the scissors before giving him her attention. Emery's eyes sparkled with amusement. Had she done something funny?

"I've determined that I will teach you to cheat at cards for the day's first lesson," Emery announced.

Ceony dropped her scissors. "I knew you were cheating!"

"Astute, but not astute enough," the paper magician replied, tapping his index finger against the side of his head. "Unless you can tell me how I did it."

"A Location spell of sorts?"

He smiled. "Of sorts. Come." He motioned with his hand.

Grabbing Fennel by his belly so he wouldn't trample the paper doll, Ceony followed Emery into the hallway, shut her door firmly, and set the dog down. Fennel sniffed the floorboards before discovering something interesting in the bathroom, and vanished from sight.

In the library, Emery sat on the floor by the table littered with neat stacks of paper, each a different color and thickness. He set his Folding board down in front of him, then pulled an ordinary stack of playing cards from an inner pocket of his coat.

Ceony sat across from him—the position she took for most of their lessons. Emery shuffled the cards rather expertly, which made her wonder what sort of employment he had taken before becoming a Folder. Her journey through his heart hadn't revealed those secrets, and so she decided it best not to ask.

"You remember the File-location spell I taught you, yes?" he asked.

Ceony did, as she remembered nearly everything that occurred in her life, whether she wanted to or not. For the most part, her photographic memory was a gift. Emery had taught her that spell the day after his recovery from losing his heart—the same day Ceony had begun calling him by his first name.

She recited the lesson. "So long as I have made physical contact with the papers in question, I can use a 'sort' command and then recite, verbatim, the written terms I am looking for."

It would have been a useful spell to know while studying for midterms at the Tagis Praff School for the Magically Inclined.

"Precisely," Emery said with a nod. "With playing cards—unless they're from a tampered deck—you can do the exact same thing. And you can assign a card a gesture instead of a name, so that the gesture will call it forward in a game. Allow me to demonstrate."

He fanned out the cards, perhaps to ensure he had, indeed, touched each of them, and then said, "Sort: King of Diamonds." One of the topmost cards pulled out of the deck toward him. He plucked it up with his other hand and turned it so Ceony could see that it was the King of Diamonds.

He then turned the card away from Ceony and, as though talking to the king himself, said, "Re-sort: Gesture," and tapped the right side of his nose once. Emery slipped the King of Diamonds back into the deck and shuffled it, dealing Ceony and himself five cards as though they were playing poker, which they had gotten into the habit of doing most Tuesday nights at a quarter past seven.

"Now," Emery said, holding up his cards. "So long as I mumble 'sort' under my breath, or somewhere where the cards can hear me, I can signal the King of Diamonds by tapping my nose. I usually find it best to say the word before I enter the room where the game is being held. But mind that you must repeat the 'sort' command for each card you intend to steal."

He coughed—Ceony thought she heard the word "sort" in the act—and tapped the side of his nose. The King of Diamonds flew out of the deck and right into Emery's waiting hand.

"How deceitful of you," Ceony said, though she couldn't help but smirk. How angry Zina would be if Ceony used this trick against her the next time they played Hearts!

"It's easiest to disguise what you're doing when you're shuffling or dealing," Emery explained, "or when your opponent is distracted by something that's cooking in the kitchen."

Ceony opened her mouth to protest, but instead closed it and shot him a disapproving look. He *had* won the game last Tuesday when Ceony had cinnamon rolls in the oven. She had been worried they would burn. Perhaps that's why Emery never kept the money she lost, regardless of the amount. The cheater.

"And how do I tamper with the deck?" she asked.

That amusement rekindled in his eyes. "A lesson for another day. I can't give away all my secrets at once," he said. He handed the deck to her, and Ceony tried the spell herself, only with the Queen of Spades. To her relief, a quick tug on her braid summoned the card on her first try.

"Now we shall see who wins at cards," Emery said, chuckling to himself. He gathered the deck and returned it to the recesses of his coat. For the next spell, he stood and retrieved two white, 8½" by 11" sheets of medium-thickness paper and set them down on the Folding board. His eyes met Ceony's for a long moment as he settled back into his seat, but Ceony couldn't read his thoughts. Emery had gotten better at hiding them these days.

"I'm going to teach you the Ripple spell, but this is one that can't be rushed," he explained, dropping his gaze to the rectangular paper in his hands. "The thickness of the paper does affect the spell—the thicker the parchment, the stronger the ripple."

"What ripple?" Ceony asked, brows drawn together. "I haven't read anything about Ripple spells."

Emery smirked and did a square Fold—a triangular Fold that formed a square when opened, after cutting off the excess paper. He sheared the excess strip off with a rotary cutter and performed a full-point Fold to turn the Folded triangle into a smaller, symmetrical triangle.

"Cutting off the excess is necessary," he explained. "Don't start with a square piece of paper. Would you hand me the ruler?"

Ceony snatched the ruler from the top drawer of the table. She heard a few pencils roll around inside the drawer as she closed it, and Emery frowned. He would probably reorganize that drawer before he left the library today. For a man who was more or less a pack rat, Emery preferred his belongings to be in perfect order. Perfect to him, at least.

Emery set the ruler down on the paper to measure the width, then laid it out across the length. "Five-eighths of an inch is the magic number. Remember that," he said. He dragged the rotary cutter across the line, but stopped short of shearing off the base of the triangle entirely. He then flipped the paper over and measured again, cutting from the other side, five-eighths of an inch up.

"Like in sewing," Ceony said, watching his hands work. Even though she would remember all the cuts, this spell would take her far longer to prepare. How did he make his measurements so quickly?

"Is it?" he asked, glancing up at her before making a third cut, flipping the triangle once more. Two more cuts, and he had an evenly sliced triangle in his hands.

He carefully unfolded it until it became a single-layered flayed square. Pinching its center, he lifted the paper up. Ceony ogled—it looked like a multi-tiered, geometric jellyfish. She didn't know any other way to describe it.

Emery stood, and Ceony followed suit.

"This is something I kept in my back pocket when I . . . aided law enforcement," he said. Ceony, of course, knew about his work hunting Excisioners, the practitioners of forbidden blood magic, but there were some things Emery just didn't like to discuss. "It's good for a distraction, or to give someone you don't like a headache."

Emery extended his arm in front of him and commanded, "Ripple," then bobbed the paper creation up and down, making it look even more like a jellyfish.

The spell blurred, but so did the rest of the library. Ceony blinked, trying to clear her vision, but the very air seemed to undulate out from the paper jellyfish, like a rock thrown into the center of a pond. The floor rolled; the bookshelves waved. The ceiling twisted and the furniture appeared to be swimming. Even Ceony's own body rippled back and forth, back and forth—

Her mind spun as vertigo assaulted her. She reached for the chair, for the table, but her hand missed and she teetered.

Emery sidestepped and caught her, one arm wrapped firmly around her shoulders. He dropped the spell, and the library reoriented itself, straight and sturdy once again.

"I should have insisted you stay seated," he said apologetically.

She shook her head, finding her feet. "No . . . it's very, uh, useful."

As her vision returned to normal, she became hyperaware of Emery's hand on her shoulder, and despite her every urge for it not to happen, her cheeks burned with a flush.

Emery's arm lingered a moment after she had steadied herself, and he seemed hesitant to remove it. Was he worried she'd fall?

Clearing his throat, Emery rubbed the back of his head. "You should practice this when you get a chance, perhaps with thinner paper to start, hmm?" He glanced toward the door, then at the table drawer containing the loose pencils. He stepped around Ceony and began reorganizing the errant drawer. "And the paper doll, of course. That should keep you busy until the tour tomorrow."

Ceony took a deep breath, hoping he didn't notice her blazing skin. "I think it will. I'll finish my work on the doll first. It's a little less jarring."

Emery nodded, and Ceony excused herself.

She settled back down on the floor of her room, leaving the door cracked open. However, as she picked up her enchanted scissors and held them to the paper doll, she found she had an especially hard time holding her hand still.

CHAPTER 3

CEONY ROSE EARLY THE next day without the help of Jonto, whom she found lurking suspiciously outside her bedroom after she had gotten dressed. She wore her red apprentice's apron over a beige blouse and navy skirt, and had pinned her hair into a bun at the nape of her neck, where the uniform top hat wouldn't disturb it. She had enough time to prepare two fried-egg sandwiches and fluff Fennel's bed before the buggy pulled up to the house, the driver casting a wary glance at the illusion of a dark mansion with broken shutters and sharp-eyed crows. He must have been new.

Emery didn't appear until the buggy honked. He looked somewhat bleary-eyed.

"You really should go to sleep earlier," Ceony commented as he locked the house. "Why did you stay up?"

"Just thinking," he said, stifling a yawn.

"About what?"

He glanced at her, paused, and smiled. "As I said, I can't give away all my secrets."

Ceony rolled her eyes and hurried to the car. "I think there's a good many hours in the *daytime* for thinking."

Emery merely smiled a second time and helped her into the cab. Once they were comfortably settled, Ceony handed him his sandwich. The man really would have starved by now had Mg. Aviosky not appointed Ceony to his stewardship. She told him so as he chewed his first bite.

"A great many things would have been different without you, that is certain," he replied.

Ceony mulled over his words for some hidden meaning, but deciphered none. Perhaps she really wasn't as astute as she should be. She wondered if there was a spell for that.

It took the buggy two hours and Ceony and Emery eleven conversation topics, ranging from Ceony's father's new job as a facilities worker for the local water treatment plant to the mating habits of honeybees, to arrive in Dartford. Ceony had never before been to Dartford. She glanced out the window as they approached, soaking in the sight of the large, industrial-looking city. Narrow, cramped-looking homes and flats occupied both sides of nearly every street, and various factories, warehouses, and sparse trees lined the city's perimeter. Dartford also had a very wide river with a port. Leaning forward, Ceony closed her eyes and held her breath as the buggy drove over a long suspended bridge, trying to block out all thoughts about the miles and miles of water beneath her. Emery placed a hand on her back for comfort, which he did not remove even after the buggy found solid land. Ceony made no comment, letting herself enjoy the subtle warmth of his fingers.

The driver pulled into a wide square paved with cobblestones, parking in a free spot amid a long line of automobiles and one unhitched carriage. When Ceony stepped out and looked for the paper mill, she saw only more flats, a butcher shop, a bookshop, a

Polymaking—plastics—studio, and some sort of foreign-foods grocery store, all more squat and less colorful than similar buildings in the capital. Only the bank building reached more than one story high.

A breeze swept by, and the hairs on the back of her neck stood on end. She turned around and scanned the narrow street behind her, but saw only businessmen on their way to work and a small flock of flying mail birds, enchanted by some other Folder in a nearby city. Odd—for a moment, Ceony had experienced the distinct sensation of being watched.

"Where's the mill?" Ceony asked after Emery paid the driver and began walking toward the square.

"It's on the east side," he answered. He jutted his chin forward, toward a short, faded red bus parked in the square. "The shuttle will take you there."

Ceony paused. "Just me?"

Emery smiled, and Ceony spied mischief in his green eyes. "It's a rather dreadful tour, and the place doesn't smell too pleasant, either. I'm going to pass on this one."

Ceony frowned. "You make it sound so exciting. Can't I just read a book about it and skip?"

"Ceony, Ceony," he said. "You do not yet know the marvels that wood chips and pulp have in store for you. There *will* be a test. This visit is a requirement of the Board of Education for Folders—elective credit for anyone else. As I told you, Magician Aviosky specifically requested your presence."

Ceony pulled her top hat down farther on her head. "There's a special place in heaven for people like you."

Emery laughed and clapped a hand on her shoulder.

"Ceony!" sang out a familiar voice.

Ceony looked toward the shuttle and spied Delilah, Mg. Aviosky's apprentice, hurrying toward her. Emery quickly withdrew his hand from Ceony's shoulder and stepped aside as the women greeted each other.

Delilah grabbed Ceony by the arms and kissed both her cheeks—French *bisous*—as she was wont to do. She was the perfect opposite of her buttoned-up mentor. While Mg. Aviosky had a rather uptight and proper demeanor, Delilah bubbled inside and out, and wore a smile that refused to ever leave her perfectly oval face. She had curled her sunny-blond hair, cut into a bob, and wore a sky-blue sundress beneath her apprentice's apron. Ceony wasn't tall, but Delilah stood a good two inches shorter.

"What are you doing here?" Ceony asked, watching from the corner of her eye as Mg. Aviosky approached Emery. "You're studying glass!"

"Magician Aviosky says it's proper to be well versed in all the materials," Delilah said with a slight French lilt, her voice reminiscent of chiming bells. "She said you'd be coming. You don't mind, do you?"

Ceony laughed. "Why would I mind? But it doesn't look like it will be a very big group."

Indeed, other than Magicians Aviosky and Thane and the bus driver, only three other apprentices—all male—had gathered by the bus, each wearing a long red vest instead of an apron. Ceony recognized two of them from her graduating class: George, a stocky man whose rimless glasses were propped on a short nose, and Dover, whose curly dark hair and tan skin had always won him the attention of Ceony's female classmates in school. Ceony suspected their attention was why it had taken Dover the full three years to receive his diploma from Tagis Praff.

Delilah took Ceony by the hand and pulled her over to the bus. She greeted all three boys and introduced Ceony to the one that she hadn't previously met. He was a tall, lanky fellow who reminded

Ceony of Prit from Emery's high school—the aspiring Folder whom Emery had bullied—except that he was a Pyre, a fire magician.

Delilah practically cooed Dover's name, but he didn't seem to mind. It surprised Ceony to learn that, like herself, both Dover and George had been assigned to paper, and George had obviously not come to terms with that fact.

"What a waste of time," he grumbled, leaning back against the bus and folding his arms loosely over his chest. "Maybe if we all hold hands and stay quiet, someone will give us lollipops at the end of this nonsense."

"A sour one for you," Ceony quipped, then flushed upon hearing her own words. She had been spending far too much time around Emery. George's ensuing scowl only punctuated that thought, though Dover turned away to hide a chuckle.

"It will be splendid," Delilah said, hanging off Ceony's right arm, "and great exercise, besides. I've always wondered how paper is made."

"Deforestation," George replied. Dover laughed, his perfect curls quivering with the effort. Clemson, the Pyre, merely scratched the back of his head.

Mg. Aviosky clapped her hands and said, "Everyone onto the shuttle. We are sending you without chaperone because you are adults; please remember that during your tour. The shuttle will meet you at the south entrance to the mill at noon. Don't be tardy. Your participation in this event *will* be recorded for your permanent record."

George cursed under his breath. Ceony met Emery's eyes and shrugged, then allowed Delilah to lead her onto the bus.

———

To Ceony's dismay, the Dartford Paper Mill really did smell awful—something like overcooked broccoli with a touch of morning breath.

Three buildings, squished together, comprised the factory itself. Seven stories tall, they were built to look like an even mix between a dormitory and a prison. The first six floors were striped with rows of evenly spaced rectangular windows, and the first and third buildings boasted a huge smokestack each, which billowed white, broccoli-scented steam into the air, making it feel especially humid. Part of the large river Ceony had ridden across earlier flowed behind the factory, turning various wheels and powering generators.

Their small tour group gathered together by the side of the shuttle. For the second time that day, Ceony felt as though someone was watching her. Gooseflesh sprang up on her arms, but none of the other apprentices seemed to notice—their attention was focused on the mill. Perhaps being in a new city had heightened her paranoia.

"I think it could look quite nice with some curtains," Delilah suggested.

"And some perfume," Ceony added. Still, she imagined that all the paper she had Folded these last three months must have come from this mill, so that meant something. Without this factory, she would be out of a job.

A tall woman in a purple jacket and an alarmingly short skirt that barely covered her knees appeared from inside the first building just as the shuttle drove off. Her dark hair was pulled back into a tight bun, and her eyelids were lined perfectly with kohl. She cradled a clipboard in the nook of her left elbow.

"Hello, hello," she said, counting each head with a bob of her finger. She took dainty steps around the pebble-strewn road. "Seems we're missing a few. Will they be on their way?"

Ceony glanced around her. "I think this is it."

"Oh. Well, all right. Still a decent group." The woman nodded. "My name is Miss Johnston, and I'll be your tour guide today. Please stay together as a group, and don't touch anything unless instructed to do so. If we can do this, the tour will move along swiftly."

George mumbled something under his breath, but Ceony didn't catch it. Likely for the best. She found herself disliking the man just a little bit more every time he opened his mouth.

Miss Johnston scribbled something onto her clipboard. "This way, follow me," she said as she led them into the first building, over a path of old stonework that had been repaired several times over with mismatching mortar. The single door into the factory was tucked under a faded brick arch, and Miss Johnston continued to chatter as the apprentices entered the building single file. "Sir John Spilman built the first paper mill in Dartford in 1588. The Dartford Paper Mill was initially founded and built by the London Paper Mills Company in 1862 after excise duty on paper was abolished. Then it was restructured in 1889. The paper mill helped industrialize Dartford, which was traditionally a hub for chalk mining, lime burning, the wool industry, and other forms of agriculture."

Delilah leaned close to Ceony and asked, "What's lime burning?"

Ceony shrugged.

They walked into a large reception foyer with green and gray floor tiling and very sparse furniture. A great many potted plants, ranging from petunias to leafy ferns, occupied every corner and cranny. Ceony spied no electric wires—all the light emanated from the tall, age-stained windows over the door. To her surprise, the broccoli smell diminished somewhat in this foyer. That, or Ceony's nose had grown accustomed to it.

A secretary behind a high beige desk glanced up at the group as it entered, but the apprentices didn't hold her interest for long.

"Back here are meeting rooms for our employees," Miss Johnston said, walking backward and gesturing to two unpainted doors on the far side of the room, half-hidden by a wild-looking fern. "As you follow me into this hallway, you'll hear the water race beneath your feet. The mill pumps water from the river through a half dozen Smelted turbines beneath the factory, which power our newest machines, all of which were made right here in England. The Dartford Paper Mill prides itself on keeping all its affairs native."

As the tour continued, each ensuing room required more explanation than the last on how the different machines worked, what each employee did, and the history behind anything and everything in view. They walked through the large collection room that made up the entire back half of the first building, where logs that had been carried in by boat were ground in a wood chipper before being sent to the pulp room. Though Miss Johnston kept the tour group far away from the chipping itself, Ceony still had to cover her ears. She couldn't hear Miss Johnston's endless lecture on the workings of the mill until they reached the pulp room, where the smell of broccoli and unbrushed teeth grew so strong Ceony would have gagged had Delilah not handed her a spare handkerchief to cover her nose with.

Unfortunately, most of the interesting parts of the mill, such as the forming and pressing sections, lingered far behind the yellow paint lines on the floor that dictated where tour groups were allowed to walk. Rows of boxes and half-empty shelves blocked the machinery, which Ceony would actually have enjoyed seeing.

Miss Johnston led them through the machine room, of which Ceony saw only a corner; the warehouse, which stood nearly the size of the wood-chipping room, but with more shelves and less light; and a room called the "dynamo and engine," which processed so much of that bitter paper smell that Ceony's eyes watered. Miss Johnston had just begun discussing the agitators and stuff chests when another employee—a young man in a smock—approached her from the left and whispered in her ear. Ceony stepped forward and strained to listen, but all she heard was "just now" and "suspicious." Still, the latter word piqued her interest.

The man left and Ceony raised her hand to ask after him, but Miss Johnston waved the question away and said, "I apologize for the inconvenience, but it seems we're experiencing some technical difficulties, which means this tour group will need to evacuate. If you'll follow me back through the warehouse, I'll have you exit out the west door. Hopefully this won't take long, and we can continue your tour. Again, my apologies."

George smacked his palm against his forehead, but the group followed Miss Johnston in silence back through the warehouse, which of course bore yellow tourist lines clear to the rusted, windowless door.

Ceony grabbed Delilah's wrist and pulled her toward the back of the group. "Did you hear what he said?" she whispered.

Delilah shook her head, tickling Ceony's nose with her curls. "I didn't. You?"

"Something suspicious. I mean, he said 'suspicious.' And something about 'just now.' What could go wrong in a paper mill that would cause them to stop the tour? Bad pulp?"

Delilah shrugged. "Big businesses always have certain protocols for things like tour groups and emergency preparation. My pa works for Stanton Automobile, and there are all sorts of weird rules about what to do when something goes wrong. It usually just results in a lot of overtime."

Ceony cringed at the idea of working overtime in a paper mill, but said nothing more on the subject.

Miss Johnston left the group outside on a stretch of trampled grass not far from the river and disappeared back through the door. Clemson tested the handle but found it locked.

"Curious," he said. It was the first word Ceony had heard him speak. The lanky man released the handle and said nothing more.

Letting out a sigh, Ceony took in her surroundings. She could hear the river churning at the back of the mill, and a gravel road wound around the side of the building to its front. A little farther out grew clusters of aspen trees and uncut crabgrass; she headed toward them with Delilah, the afternoon sun peeking out from behind wispy clouds. The others followed at a slow pace, George grumbling as he went.

"I think we should do lunch sometime soon, Ceony," Delilah said with a grin. She handled inconvenience so well. Ceony envied that about her.

"I agree," Ceony said, "but it's on your schedule. Em—Magician Thane is fairly lenient about my time off."

"Oh, I think tomorrow would suit just right," Delilah said, clapping her hands together. "Magician Aviosky has a full day booked at the school, what with the new year starting soon, so I'll only have personal study to complete. Where shall we go?"

Ceony paused under a tree some fifty feet from the paper mill and leaned against its white, scarred trunk. "Do you like fish? St. Alban's Salmon Bistro at Parliament Square has really good bisque. I've tried to copy it before, but I can never get it right."

"Oh, I love St. Alban's," Delilah said with a wave of her hand. "Their bread is heavenly. Tomorrow at noon, then? I can meet you outside the statue of—"

Delilah's lips kept moving, but a loud *boom!* from behind her completely enveloped her words. Ceony felt the explosion through the ground, up her legs, and in her very heart. The leaves overhead rattled, and two starlings took to the sky.

Then Ceony saw the fire.

Flames soared upward from the first and second buildings of the paper mill like an erupting volcano, spitting chunks of debris and ash higher than the smokestacks' steam. They engulfed half the building; the heat hit in a wall-like wave a moment later, pulling beads of sweat from her skin.

"Run!" she shouted, barely able to hear her own voice. She grabbed Delilah and pulled her in the opposite direction of the mill. Clemson was nowhere in sight, but George and Dover had already taken off, and she raced after them. A piece of debris slammed into a tree not ten feet to her left, splitting it in two.

Something whistled, and a second, smaller explosion sang through the air. Ceony turned just in time to see a massive chunk of factory wall hurtling toward her.

Clemson appeared out of nowhere and ran toward it, rubbing his hands together. Ceony screamed, but the man shouted "Deflect!" and shot a giant fireball into the debris, knocking it away. Instead of smashing into Ceony, it soared over the trees and landed in the river with a giant splash.

Delilah started to cry.

"Thank you!" Ceony shouted, but Clemson just shoved them forward, dropping a spent match in the process. Ceony didn't need any reminder of the danger they were in. She ran as fast as her legs would carry her, which turned out to be much faster than what Delilah could manage. Ceony refused to let go of the Gaffer apprentice's hand, and half-dragged her over a small hill toward the street the shuttle had used to get to the factory. Dover and George had already reached it by the time they got there, and were standing with a small collection of awestruck bystanders. When Ceony finally stopped, chest heaving with each breath, Delilah buried herself into Ceony's collar and continued to sob. Clemson approached cautiously, but a shake of Ceony's head suggested he stay away, and he did. Ceony patted Delilah's back in a meager attempt to console her and stared at the pillar of dark-gray smoke churning up from the paper mill. What had happened? What had gone wrong?

She tensed as another thought occurred to her: Of all the employees Miss Johnston had pointed out to them on the tour, how many had escaped in time?

The air soured with the smell of ashes and soot. More and more people collected on the street to ogle the catastrophe until the police arrived and started pushing everyone back. The first group of policemen ran straight up to the mill; the second worked on crowd control.

Her skin prickled again with that feeling of being watched. She searched the crowd as best she could with Delilah clinging to her, but so many people surrounded them . . .

Across the street, however, one person did stand out. He wore normal clothes, but his dark skin contrasted with the rest of the bystanders. He was a tall man—Indian, or perhaps Arab. His dark eyes met hers, and then the crowd filled in and he vanished from sight.

Ceony sucked in a deep breath. What decent person would look askance at a foreigner, even if he had been looking her way? Plenty of foreigners lived in England. Delilah was a foreigner, for heaven's sake. Ceony's mother would be appalled if she knew Ceony suspected a man merely because he was different.

Ceony looked around once more for the others, but Clemson, Dover, and George had either left or gotten lost in the throng. She handed Delilah a handkerchief to dry her eyes and, heart buzzing, approached the closest policeman.

"Excuse me," she said. The man glanced her way before returning his gaze to the burning paper mill.

Ceony removed her hat and waved it back and forth, demanding his attention. "My friend and I are magicians' apprentices; we were on tour when the building exploded."

His eyes narrowed. "We'll need to question you."

"Yes, that's fine," Ceony said, raising her voice to be heard over the people, "but we need to return to Town Centre and find our teachers. They'll be worried, and we're not from around here. Please."

The policeman rolled his lips together for a long moment before nodding. "One moment," he said. He stepped over to his comrade and muttered something to him. The other policeman nodded and retrieved a pre-animated paper messenger bird from the trunk of his automobile. After scribbling a missive on it, he released it into the wind, but it flew away from Town Centre. Perhaps it was a call for reinforcements.

More police arrived on the scene about a quarter of an hour later, many on horseback, and one of them offered Ceony and Delilah a ride back to Town Centre. Ceony thanked him profusely, and Delilah even offered him money, which he didn't accept. Trying to calm herself, Ceony led the way into the square, searching for Emery, praying he would be nearby. If all had gone as planned, the shuttle wouldn't have dropped them off here for another hour, but it seemed inevitable that Emery and Mg. Aviosky would have noticed the commotion.

Even more people had congregated in Town Centre than at the mill, and all were gossiping about the explosion. Ceony could see the pillars of smoke from the square, dancing into the sky like poisoned clouds. She stopped and stared for a moment, holding her breath. Would they be able to put out the flames? What in the world had created a disaster of this magnitude?

She pushed through a crowd of women and a collection of schoolchildren, standing on her toes in a poor attempt to get a better view. She reached into her bag and pulled free a piece of paper to send a signal over the square—a wide-winged crane would work well for revealing her location. She searched for a decent place to Fold it, eyes scanning past the clusters of onlookers and the shop owners who stood outside their doors, pointing and chatting.

Ceony spied a flash of indigo between two newspaper boys and shoved the paper back into her bag. She motioned for Delilah to follow her and pushed forward in that direction.

She found Emery and Mg. Aviosky talking to two disgruntled police officers. Or rather, Mg. Aviosky stood by silently while Emery yelled at them.

"Then take me!" Emery shouted, a vein on the side of his forehead looking especially rigid. The skin around his eyes was flushed, and he waved his hands in the air like cleavers. "Don't you understand? She might be in there! They all might be in there. We have to go!"

"Sir," said the taller officer, "as I've already explained, we can only—"

"Emery!" Ceony shouted as she pushed past the last of the crowd. Emery whirled around at his name. "It's okay, we got out before—"

The rest of her words were cut off when Emery threw his arms around her and embraced her, sending her top hat—and her stomach—tumbling to the ground.

"Thank God," he said into her hair, squeezing her to his chest. Her blood raced through her veins faster than when the giant piece of rubble had been hurtling toward her. "Oh, Ceony, I thought . . ."

He pulled back and looked her up and down. His green eyes shined with worry and relief. This time, she had no trouble reading his mood. "Are you all right? Are you hurt?"

She shook her head, her pulse beating in her throat. "I-I'm fine, I promise. And Delilah, and the others. We left the building before . . . I don't know what happened. I don't know where Clemson and Dover and George are, but they got out, too. They were with us."

Emery heaved a long breath and closed his eyes, then tugged Ceony close again. She returned the embrace, letting her arms snake under his coat, hoping that if Emery could feel the hammering in her chest, he would attribute it to the disaster at the paper mill and not their closeness. "If it makes you feel any better," she murmured, "it really was boring, up until the end."

Emery laughed, though it was more of a nervous sound than a mirthful one. He stepped back, but kept his hands on her shoulders. "I am so sorry."

"It wasn't . . . ," she began. From the corner of her eye, she caught a glimpse of Mg. Aviosky, who was standing with Delilah. The Gaffer wore a sour expression—a frown that could mean nothing but disapproval.

Ceony flushed and pulled away from Emery. "It wasn't your fault, but there were people inside. And I don't know what happened . . ."

Her voice shook a little on those last words. She coughed to steady it.

One of the officers Emery had been arguing with stepped forward. "You were a witness?" he asked.

Ceony nodded.

"Please come with us," he said. "I'd like to ask you some questions about what you saw and where. Her, too." He gestured toward Delilah.

"Of course," Ceony said, and she felt Emery's hand clasp hers behind the shield of his coat. "Whatever is necessary."

"I'll accompany them," Emery said.

"As will I," said Mg. Aviosky. "I'm these girls' director; any involvement they have in this incident is my responsibility."

The officers nodded. "My automobile is out this way. Please."

Ceony, Emery, Delilah, and Mg. Aviosky followed the officers to their cars, and rode with them to the police station, where Ceony filed her report in the utmost detail she could muster, including the two words she had overheard whispered to Miss Johnston. *Dear God, let her be safe.*

Ceony and Emery stayed at the station until late into the night, but it seemed no one had any solid evidence as to what could have caused the explosion, short of sabotage.

But as Ceony rode in a hired buggy back through the dark roads to London, she couldn't help but wonder, *Who would want to sabotage a paper mill?*

CHAPTER 4

CEONY LAY AWAKE IN her bed, her arm splayed across her forehead to keep the morning sunlight from her eyes. Fennel whined at her from the floor, his paper tail beating a rapid rhythm against the carpet. She reached a hand toward him and stroked the top of his paper head.

In her mind she stood in front of the paper mill's three buildings, the shuttle driving away down the pebbled road behind her. Miss Johnston mumbled ahead of her. Ceony strained her memory for any forgotten details that might explain what had happened. She wished she'd paid more attention. But the police had said the explosion happened in the drying room, of all places, and Ceony's tour never reached that part of the mill. That's why the police suspected sabotage—there was nothing in the drying room that could have malfunctioned on such a large scale.

Ceony recalled the intense heat on her face as the fire soared toward the sky. She could only imagine how much hotter it must have been inside. By the time she and Emery had left the police station, fourteen casualties had already been reported. Ceony had read the list—no one with the surname "Johnston" had been on it.

Closing her eyes, Ceony replayed the explosion, the fire, the falling rubble. Thank goodness for Clemson, whose Pyre magic had saved her life. No paper spell could have rescued her from being crushed. But she hadn't included the falling rubble in her police report. Emery had been listening, and she hadn't wanted to distress him. He had been so . . . quiet. Worried about her. Ceony had been too shaken to relish the way he'd held her, but . . .

Ceony sat up and straightened the bodice of her nightgown, then moved to her desk, which sat on the opposite side of the small bedroom. In the back of the second drawer rested the fortuity box that had offered her such pleasant promises for the future. She held it for a long moment before returning it to its hiding spot. It was bad luck to read one's own fortune, and Ceony had experienced her fill of bad luck for the week.

Fennel coughed a faint bark and wagged his tail. Moments later, Ceony detected the smell of bacon wafting under her door. Had Emery decided to cook breakfast?

She glanced at her clock—ten past nine. She had slept in late today.

Quickly changing into a blouse, skirt, and a pair of stockings, Ceony went to the bathroom to brush her teeth, braid her hair, and apply her makeup. She hurried down the steep stairs that opened onto the dining room, where Emery had already loaded two plates with bacon and eggs.

"You didn't have to do this. I was up," Ceony said, though it impressed her that the bacon wasn't burned and the eggs looked perfectly sunny. Ever since being fed tuna and rice on her first day as an apprentice, Ceony had insisted on cooking every meal. After all, if not for Emery's scholarship, she would have enrolled in culinary school.

"I *am* capable of cooking," Emery said, pulling out a chair for her, "else I would have starved long ago."

Ceony smiled and settled into the seat while Emery retrieved silverware. Perhaps he had needed to cook while married to Lira. The Excisioner didn't seem like she'd be much of a cook, though Ceony wouldn't dream of asking him about it. If any topic made Emery uncomfortable, it was his ex-wife.

Ceony wondered if Lira was still as she'd left her—frozen and bleeding on the rocky beach of Foulness Island—but then Emery sat down beside her, and the memories flitted away.

He handed her a telegram.

"What's this?" she asked, unfolding it.

lets not change plans stop albans at noon stop

"It came this morning," Emery said between bites. He frowned at his eggs and reached for the pepper shaker. "I believe it's from Delilah, unless you've taken to arranging social visits with Patrice Aviosky."

His eyes shined as he chuckled at his own joke.

"I would like to meet her for lunch," Ceony said, "unless you need me here."

Emery thought for a moment, chewing, and left the table without excuse. He returned with a 9" by 14" sheet of paper, which he tore in half.

"Mimic," he told it—a spell unfamiliar to Ceony. He then haphazardly folded one half into quarters and handed it to Ceony.

"Anything you write on this will appear on my copy," he explained in an unusually protective tone. "That way, if you need anything . . . Well, it's self-explanatory."

Ceony turned the spell over in her hands. "You've never sent me out with one of these before."

"One can never be too irrational. Don't be too long. There is plenty of homework to do!"

After breakfast, Ceony headed back to her room. As she packed her purse with the Mimic spell and some spare paper, she couldn't help but feel uneasy about her situation. Three months ago, she had confessed her love for Emery while quite literally trapped in the fourth chamber of his heart. He still had not directly addressed her confession. He avoided uncomfortable subjects as a general rule, so perhaps the confession had made him uncomfortable. Ceony's cheeks burned at the thought; when she'd said the words, she hadn't believed he would remember them upon waking. And Ceony still couldn't forget Lira's cruel laughter. "*He doesn't love you,*" she'd said.

Her gaze drifted again to the second drawer in her desk. What if the fortuity box had only shown her what she *wanted* to see, and not the truth? What if she had already done something to upset that possibility of future events, leaving her longing for something that was no longer an option?

She sighed. She had only been in one previous relationship, in secondary school, and that had been much easier than this. Perhaps she should take that as a sign and give up.

Yet she couldn't give up on Emery. She knew that more surely than anything.

She loved him.

She loved his genuineness, his honesty, his cleverness, his humor and eccentricity. She loved the way his hands moved when he Folded, and the way he pursed his lips when concentrating. She loved his kindness—at least, he was always kind to her. She imagined a great number of people felt scorned by Emery Thane, or they would if they were sharp enough to notice when he mocked them. He had a very subtle way of insulting people.

Still, she wished she hadn't fallen for him as quickly as she had.

She took her safety bicycle—complete with enchanted tires that wouldn't wear—into town. She had purchased it one month into her apprenticeship after growing weary of waiting for buggies and spending large chunks of her stipend on transportation. It made for a much longer ride, but the road into the city was a peaceful one, so Ceony didn't mind. She just made sure to stay on the far side of the street, away from the narrow river running alongside it.

She found Delilah waiting outside St. Alban's Salmon Bistro, a small, redbrick shop with chocolate-colored window molds and a worn, oval sign over the window that bore a weathered blue fish. Delilah looked like her normal, chipper self. She waved broadly as Ceony parked her bicycle.

"How are you feeling?" Ceony asked once they had been seated at a small oak table near the center of the half-filled restaurant. A few couples and a family occupied the booths to their left and right. The scent of cooking fish wafted through the air; the sound of clinking dishes percussed from the kitchen. Ceony tucked her purse under the table, near her feet.

"Oh, Ceony, wasn't it just awful?" Delilah said as she glanced over the menu. Her eyes lingered for a moment before she set it down. "I kept waking up last night. Magician Aviosky cancelled all her appointments this morning and headed back to Dartford. She's all wrung up, worse than usual. Says she can't sit by while students are in danger."

"They're not still in danger, are they?" Ceony asked, hair follicles prickling.

Delilah shook her head. "Well, no, we're all fine," she said as the waiter brought their water. "The others went to a different station, is all. I don't know more than that. But I was so embarrassed. I have a spinning head, you know. I wish I could stay calm, like you."

Ceony laughed. "I don't think anyone's described me as calm before." She paused. "I don't know. I suppose after you see so much, the extraordinary starts to become more ordinary."

"Have you seen so many extraordinary things?" Delilah asked, leaning forward. "Do tell! I hope they're romantic."

Ceony blushed. "Not entirely. And perhaps I'll tell you when we're alone." She didn't think it wise to recount her Excisioner escapades in a crowded restaurant, especially since Mg. Aviosky knew very little of what had actually happened with Lira, short of what Emery had shared with Criminal Affairs.

As for Emery . . . she'd keep that to herself.

The waiter carried a small basket of bannock to their table and took their order. Delilah requested fish and chips, and Ceony asked for crab bisque. Afterward, Delilah stuck her head into the large cloth bag she had brought with her, muttered something, and then resurfaced with a compact makeup mirror. It was a beautiful object—a silver Celtic knot was welded to the top, and a seashell-shaped clasp kept it closed.

"Extraordinary like this?" she asked.

Raising her eyebrows, Ceony accepted the mirror and opened it. Only, instead of the reflection of her face, the dark eyes of a gorilla blinked back at her.

Ceony shrieked and dropped the mirror. Delilah laughed and scooped it off the table.

"How did you do that?" Ceony asked.

"It's a Choice Reflection spell," she explained. "You can make the mirror reflect whatever you picture in your head."

"With just a command," Ceony mumbled, thinking of Delilah's covert whispering. She studied the compact in Delilah's hands. There were very few spells Ceony could merely dictate to a piece of paper; Folding required just that: Folds. Preparation, foresight. Manipulation with creases and cuts. Gaffing, or glass magic, was the second quickest after fire magic. Smelting, or enchanting metal alloys, was the slowest.

Ceony tapped her fingers on the table. "It's like story illusion."

Delilah frowned. "Um, yes? I'm not sure what that is. But you face the mirror"—Delilah opened the compact and gazed into it—"and say 'choice reflection,' and think of exactly what you want—or don't want—to see."

She repeated the spell, closed her eyes, and showed Ceony the mirror again. This time Ceony wasn't even *in* the reflection. Instead she could see the broad-shouldered man who sat alone by the window behind her. Clearly interested in their conversation, he craned his head for a better look.

Delilah cancelled the spell, snapped the mirror shut, and held it out to her. "A late birthday gift for you. Sorry I didn't wrap it, but I thought the trick would be fun."

Ceony's lips parted as she looked at the mirror. "Oh, Delilah, it's so pretty. You didn't have to—"

"Take it, take it," she laughed, shaking the compact at her.

Ceony took it with a smile and traced the Celtic ornament with her fingers as she slipped it into her purse. "Thank you."

"My birthday is in December," Delilah said matter-of-factly. "Don't forget."

"December eleventh," Ceony said. "I won't."

Seeming content, Delilah relaxed into her chair, took a sip of water, and said, "Ceony, are you in love?"

Ceony, who had also taken a sip of water, sputtered as she struggled to swallow it. "Wh-What?"

"You just have this faraway, airy look lately. Like on the shuttle. And on your bike."

"You mean the way you look when you're around Dover?" Ceony teased.

Delilah stuck out her tongue. "I think he likes me. At least, he went out of his way to send me a paper dove after the dreadful thing with the mill. He's two years younger, but he doesn't *look* younger. That's all that really matters."

Their meals arrived, and between bites the two of them chatted about the paper mill, Ceony's paper doll, and the new feather fashion in women's hats. When Big Ben, north of Parliament Square, chimed one thirty, Delilah snatched up her paper napkin and dabbed her lips.

"I'm so sorry, Ceony," she said, "but I told Magician Aviosky I'd attend a glassblowing appointment on her behalf at two, since she's in Dartford. You'll forgive me?"

Ceony waved a hand. "It's fine. I need to head back, too."

Delilah circled the table and kissed both of Ceony's cheeks. "Let's do it again sometime." She dropped a few shillings on the table and hurried out the front door.

Tilting her bowl, Ceony scraped out the last of her bisque, but the chair across from her rattled before she could bring the spoon to her lips.

A broad-shouldered man sat down in the seat Delilah had just vacated. Ceony recognized him as the person she'd seen in the mirror.

She lowered her bowl.

Something about the man seemed familiar, but Ceony had a hard time pinpointing what. He looked to be in his early forties, with a well-built form and light, almost ginger-colored hair. Narrow, expressionless gray eyes watched her beneath thick eyebrows and a creased forehead.

"Can I help you?" Ceony asked.

The faintest grin spread just above his broad chin.

Ceony's breath caught as her memory settled. She *knew* that chin. The nose looked wrong—a fake—but she remembered that chin, those eyes. She had seen them on a wanted poster at the post office. She had watched them lurk behind bars in the second chamber of Emery's heart.

She had seen this man in the distance as she stood on the shore of Foulness Island.

Her mouth went dry, and her tongue hardened to a brick in her mouth. She gripped her napkin—her paper napkin.

Mind spinning, she managed to say, "You're Grath Cobalt."

The most renowned Excisioner in England, if not all of Europe.

She tried to slide her chair back—she couldn't let him touch her!—but Grath hooked his foot around its front left leg.

No one in the restaurant noticed anything out of the ordinary. Not as far as Ceony could tell. She dared to glance at the main entrance to the restaurant, then to the back door behind her and to the left. What would he do if she screamed? He sat so close, and it would only take one touch for a spell . . .

She smoothed the napkin in her lap, keeping her eyes on Grath as she formed a half-point Fold.

"I'm impressed you recognize me," Grath said with a lopsided smirk. His long canines made him look like a cat. "Smart girl."

"Posters of you are everywhere," Ceony replied, trying to sound nonchalant. She glanced at the waiter three tables over.

Grath yanked her chair forward. "Eyes on me, sweetheart. Let's get this chat out of the way. I have places to go."

Ceony drew in a shaky breath and carefully maneuvered her clammy fingers over her lap. Full-point Fold, duck Fold.

"It took a while to track you down," Grath said, playing with Delilah's fork. It looked so tiny in his giant hands. "All I knew to look for was a redheaded girl with strange magic. And you turned out to be Emery Thane's apprentice, of all people. How is the bugger? Still kicking, I hear."

Ceony said nothing. She kept her gaze fixed on Grath's cool stare.

Grath chuckled, but his smile vanished too soon. He leaned forward, dangerously close. "I want you to tell me what you did to Lira."

Adrenaline made Ceony's skin prickle. "I-I didn't do anything."

Grath slammed his fist on the table, rattling the dishes and earning a few curious looks from the other patrons. It took all Ceony's willpower not to jump. "You're not in any position to lie to me, Ceony Maya Twill. What strange sorcery did you cast on her?"

"I did nothing strange," she lied. Four-corners Fold, and she flipped the napkin over. "I'm a Folder, that's all."

"What spell?"

Ceony sucked in a long breath, fingers prodding the napkin to check its alignment. "I won't tell you," she whispered. "The world is better off without her. The sooner—"

Grath jerked her chair to the left. Ceony winced, but made her last Fold without flinching.

"You think I care about the people here?" he growled, barely above a whisper. "You think I care if they have to watch me slice the skin from your bones? They're cowards, Ceony. They'll run the minute blood spills. And I will spill *all* of it, drop by drop, until you tell me what I want to know.

"Or maybe I'll start with them," he said, cocking his head toward a family of four in the corner. They had an adolescent girl and a young boy with them. "Do you know how strong a child's heart is, Ceony? The sort of spells I could cast with one?"

Ceony shut her eyes for a moment. Too many memories, things she wished she could unsee, came flooding up at those words—the gaping hole in Emery's chest as he collapsed to the floor, his heart clutched in Lira's hands; the pressure of the bloody, sweltering walls of Emery's heart pressing against her on all sides; the sight of harvested corpses strewn across the floor of a warehouse storage room. She coaxed them down, burying them deep within her mind. Hadn't Delilah just called her calm? *Be calm*, she pleaded to herself.

"All right," she said, careful. "You want to know how I froze Lira?"

Grath knit his fingers under his chin, waiting.

Ceony drew another deep breath. "It started with this."

She dropped the rhombus-shaped napkin on the middle of the table and whispered, "Burst."

The napkin began to vibrate rapidly. First Grath looked confused. Then his eyes widened.

In one movement, Ceony twisted her chair away from the Excisioner's foot and leapt from the table, bolting for the back door.

The Burst spell exploded.

The explosion wasn't as strong as when Ceony had used the spell against Lira, since this one had been made with thin napkin paper, but it was large enough to send dishes flying and chunks of table scattering. Large enough to burn anyone who came too close, even an Excisioner like Grath.

Ceony didn't survey the damage. She slammed her body into the back door and bolted into the sunlit street.

She sprinted across the road, earning an angry yell from a driver, and took a sharp corner around a bank and out of Parliament Square. Her heart raced with her legs as she rushed down one street and dodged between a hotel and a rug shop, jumping over a busted curb. Distance. She needed to get as far away from Grath as she could, put as many things between them as possible.

Emery! She reached for the Mimic spell only to realize she'd left it at the restaurant, along with her purse, mirror, and bike. She had no way to contact him.

Delilah! But which glassblower had she gone to? She could be anywhere by now.

Ceony paused at an intersection between a single-story pet-supply store and a two-story antique shop, panting, peering through the mass of people who were blissfully unaware of the danger in their midst. Grath didn't care about people—he had said as much. She needed to get away from the crowd.

She heard shouts behind her and ran to the right, nearly knocking over a man laden with groceries. Her lungs began to burn as she pushed past him and kept running. *Aviosky. Magician Aviosky lives in the city.* If Ceony could round the next block and make it over the bridge, perhaps she could reach—

She took another sharp right and collided into something solid—a huge man in a brown vest and brown trousers. The impact sent her toppling backward. She landed flat on her rump.

Stars filled her eyes.

"Miss!" the man exclaimed. "Are you all right? I'm terribly sorry! Here, let me help you up."

He extended his thick hand, which was even bigger than Grath's. Ceony clasped it, and the man pulled her up so swiftly her vision swam.

"Thank you," she mumbled between breaths as the world settled back into place. She blinked at the man before her. He appeared to be in his late twenties and would have looked rather portly if not for his height. His mousy-brown hair had been well oiled and slicked to one side, and his brown eyes—

Ceony recognized him.

"I . . . Langston!"

The man looked surprised. "Have we met?"

They hadn't, not really, but Ceony knew Langston—Emery's first apprentice—from the first chamber of Emery's heart. Langston had helped Emery build Jonto.

And though he had more girth than muscle, he was about twice Grath's size.

"My name is Ceony," she rushed. "I'm Magician Thane's apprentice and I'm incredibly lost. Please, please, can you help me get home?"

Langston blinked several times, clearly confused by this turn of events, but nodded. "Of course—I have an auto parked just a few streets down. It won't be a problem; my meeting was cancelled anyway."

Langston offered his arm, which Ceony gratefully—and desperately—accepted.

As they walked she dared to spy over her shoulder, but she saw no sign of Grath Cobalt behind her.

CHAPTER 5

EMERY WAS KNEELING OUTSIDE "gardening" when Ceony and Langston stepped through the illusion that masked the paper magician's house. He had positioned himself outside the curving garden of meticulously crafted paper flowers, and seemed to be replacing all the red, tulip-shaped flower heads with blue, lily-shaped ones. Fennel chewed on the discarded spells as Emery worked, crumpling them in his paper mouth and then spitting the balls into an overturned trash receptacle. The paper dog yipped at the sight of Ceony.

"Langston?" Emery asked as he stood and brushed off his slacks. "I didn't expect your company today."

Before the younger Folder could answer, however, Ceony blurted, "Grath Cobalt is in the city, and I think I've blown up my wallet."

Emery's expression turned to stone. Even his eyes darkened, reminding Ceony all too well of the third chamber of his heart, where she'd seen his failures and heartbreaks. His darkness. "Are you sure?" he asked, but it didn't sound like a question. In fact, the words sounded . . . threatening.

Ceony nodded. "I know him, from . . . from before," she said, eyes dropping to Emery's chest for just a moment. "He spoke to me at the bistro."

Emery's skin grayed. "Both of you come inside," he said, turning from the garden and crushing a blue lily under his foot, "and let's talk."

———

Langston headed for the crowded sitting room and sunk into the middle cushion of the sofa to make himself comfortable, but Ceony marched down the hallway to the kitchen. It was where she often went to think over difficult things. Needing something to busy her hands, she stoked the stove and filled the teakettle with water, then sifted through the cupboards until she found dried peppermint leaves. She divided them into three ceramic cups, despite not wanting tea herself. She doubted Emery would want any, either; in fact, he came into the kitchen before the water had a chance to boil. She took the kettle off the stove anyway.

He stood behind her while she poured the hot water into the teacups. "Tell me what happened."

"No one got hurt, I don't think," she said. *No one but Grath*, she supposed. She had made the spell small enough to avoid hurting any of the other patrons, but it must have scared half the life out of them.

Emery pulled the kettle from her hands and set it on the counter, then grasped her shoulders and turned her toward him. "Ceony," he said, enunciating each syllable, despite a hush in his voice. He stooped until his vivid green eyes peered straight into hers. "Tell me what happened."

Ceony related her lunch date with Delilah, Grath's poor disguise, and the Excisioner's demands regarding Lira. Emery's lips thinned more and more with every sentence, but they parted when Ceony mentioned the man's threats.

Perhaps she shouldn't have repeated the conversation verbatim.

Saying Grath's words with her own lips somehow gave them more weight. She turned to the dining room wall where Lira had pinned Emery without hands and stolen his heart. She thought of the corpses trapped in the back room of the meatpacking warehouse, perhaps the most horrifying image Ceony had beheld inside Emery's heart. She thought of the uneasy warmth that had flowed through her skin when Lira had grabbed her and started to chant.

She shivered.

"I would have used the Mimic spell to tell you, but it was in my purse. I only ran into Langston afterward. I didn't want to involve him, but I'm afraid it's too late for that."

"I doubt he'll become a target," Emery said, solemn. "But let's hope Grath didn't see him, or doesn't care. He tends to choose very specific quarries."

He took Ceony's hand, which calmed her nerves and excited a different set of them, and led her to the living room. He released her before they reached Langston's line of sight.

Emery asked for his former apprentice's story, but Langston didn't have much to add, having only seen Ceony after her confrontation with Grath.

"If I could bother you with a favor, Langston," Emery said when the younger Folder finished, "I'd like you to file a police report for me."

Langston pulled a sheet of paper from his breast pocket and plucked a pen from a narrow canister on the end table, enchanting it so that it would transcribe everything Ceony said as she related her tale for a second time. Langston looked ghostly when Ceony recounted Grath's threats, but he said nothing, either out of politeness or because he didn't want to ruin the Transcription spell.

The story told, Langston folded the transcription into eighths and slipped it into the pocket of his vest.

"I'll see that it's done," he promised, smoothing the sides of his mousy-brown hair. The sofa creaked as he rose. "I'm glad I ran into you when I did, Ceony. I'd hate to think . . . but take care." To Emery, he said, "You know where to reach me."

Emery nodded and saw Langston to the door. He then woke Jonto and sent him outside to clean up the deadheaded flowers.

"Grath was our neighbor when we lived in Berkshire," Emery said as he shut the front door. "He went by the name Gregory then. Worked as a rug salesman, of all things. I used to have some of his merchandise in this room"—he gestured weakly around him—"but I discarded them some time ago."

Ceony only nodded. She didn't blame him, of course. Emery had many reasons to hate Grath Cobalt. While Ceony had never found solid proof for it in his heart, she suspected Lira had begun . . . *associating* . . . with Grath long before Emery filed any divorce papers. It shocked Ceony that Emery's heart hadn't been in pieces long before Lira wrenched it from his chest.

She rubbed her forehead. Berkshire. Ceony supposed the old house from Emery's memories had been located there.

"Do you think he's responsible for what happened at the paper mill?" she asked. Her heart twisted at the thought. Could the explosion at the paper mill—and all the resulting deaths—be her fault?

Leaning against the wall, Emery folded his arms and answered, "Possibly. But Grath doesn't like to bring attention to himself; he's too smart for that. Explosions aren't his style. If I were to link the two cases together, I'd pin the mill on Saraj." He frowned. "I wonder if they're still working together . . ."

Ceony swallowed her anxiety. "Saraj?"

She *had* seen two people heading toward Foulness Island in that boat before she left with Emery's heart.

Emery waved a dismissive hand. "Another Excisioner who has some camaraderie with Grath when the mood strikes . . . but it doesn't matter." He ran his fingers back through his hair. "This is getting complicated."

Ceony wanted to ask more, but the way Emery drooped made her want to lock the subject in a cellar and bury the key. Instead, she placed a hand on his folded forearms. "It will work out, one way or another. It always does."

Emery chuckled. "I find it odd that you're trying to reassure me when *you're* the one in trouble, my dear." The mirth faded from his voice. "But let us hope Grath is the only Excisioner in town. I really wanted to be done with the lot of them."

As Emery often did when stressed, he went to work. He pulled a thick, yard-long roll of paper out of his office and dragged it into the front yard, then instructed Ceony to get so many 8½" by 11" and 6" by 6" sheets of paper from the rolls behind his desk. He worked without his board and with a pair of scissors that had materialized from somewhere within his indigo coat. It didn't take long for Ceony to realize he was changing the wards about the house. Not wanting to interrupt, she sat on the porch with Fennel. When Emery did need a hand, he had Jonto assist him.

He moved with remarkable swiftness, and his work was so intricate and complicated that Ceony wondered if she really could earn her magicianship in the minimum two years, for she obviously had much left to learn. Emery tore here, snipped there, and Folded long fan Folds and quad Folds back and forth in seemingly random places.

When he had finished, he finally addressed Ceony. "Would you go outside the gate and tell me what you see?"

Ceony followed the narrow pathway from the porch to the gate and stepped out onto the lane, passing the perimeter of Emery's paper illusions. Looking back at the cottage, she didn't see a dark, haunted mansion, but a barren landscape, complete with tumble-weed and cracked, sandy earth. Emery had made the house completely invisible.

After a moment, Emery passed through the spell and stood out with her, his coat tossed over his shoulder from the heat. He tapped two fingers on his chin and frowned, more in his eyes than in his mouth, which worried Ceony. He said nothing, but it was clear he wasn't satisfied.

Ceony made his second-favorite meal, shepherd's pie, for dinner—his first favorite required halibut, of which they had none—and even prepared a gooseberry cobbler for dessert. Emery thanked her, and his words were sincere, but she could tell his mind lingered elsewhere. Wherever the paper magician went on days like this, Ceony knew she couldn't follow.

His thoughts still drifted the following day, so Ceony let him be and worked on her studies, reading *The Art of Eastern Origami* and working on her paper doll. It wasn't until evening that Emery's mind stopped its wandering, and he announced, just as Ceony pulled a salad bowl for dinner from the cupboard, that they were leaving the cottage.

"Leaving?" Ceony asked, nearly dropping the bowl. "Why?"

"Isn't it obvious?" Emery asked. But it wasn't. His tone concealed his thoughts and his gaze was once again impenetrable. "Grath is here, and if you're his target—which seems to be the case—he's not leaving anytime soon. I spent years hunting this man, Ceony. Even when he knew we were closing in on him, he never took the easy way out. He always . . . finished his business first."

His voice drooped at the end of the sentence.

Ceony clasped her hands to her chest and whispered, "Was he at the warehouse?"

She thought of the rotting bodies harvested for their blood and organs. Had Grath's hands torn those people apart?

Her mind tried to bring up the crisp images of the bodies left rotting there, but Ceony squeezed her eyes shut and pushed them away. She returned the bowl to its cupboard, having lost her appetite.

"Him, among others," Emery said, perhaps more solemn than she had ever heard him. It made her heart break in two. She took a step toward him, but stopped herself. Perhaps, in this instance, it would be better not to overstep the bounds of an apprentice.

"It's safer this way," Emery said, meeting her eyes. "I'm easy to find, even with the wards. Unfortunately, the Cabinet requires open knowledge of all magician residences, which makes it incredibly hard for a man to be a recluse when he wants to be, and I don't trust the Cabinet's internal security. We'll head for the city. Easy to get lost there."

"But you hate the city."

Emery sighed. "But I hate the city. I'll telegram for a buggy. You should pack. Lightly. I don't know how long we'll be gone, but we should stay mobile."

"I'm sorry about all of this—"

"We should invest in one of those telephones," Emery said over her, flipping on his selective listening like a light switch. He hummed to himself and left the room.

Upstairs, Ceony pulled her suitcase out from under her bed, but determined it was too large to carry with her should she need to leave anywhere in a hurry. Instead she opened it and pulled out the cloth bag she had taken with her when she fell into Emery's heart. It had required a great deal of scrubbing and mending, and two patches, but she couldn't bring herself to replace it. It felt too sentimental to toss away.

She folded one change of clothes—she could wash what she was wearing if need be—and set them in the base of the bag, followed by her makeup kit and hygiene products, and her book on origami, spare paper protected under its back cover. Fennel began sniffing about the bag, which he seemed to recognize from their adventure.

Ceony picked him up and hugged him as tightly as one could hug a dog made of paper.

"If you want to come with me, I'll need you to fold up like before, boy. Just for a little while."

Fennel wagged his tail and huffed.

"Fold up."

Fennel licked her with his dry paper tongue, then stuck his head down and his back legs forward so Ceony could fold him into a somewhat flat, lopsided pentagon. She slid him carefully into the bag, making sure to secure him, and lifted the strap onto her shoulder.

She took one last view of her room, frowned, and headed downstairs.

Whatever happened, at least Emery would be with her.

When the buggy arrived at a quarter to nine, the last tendrils of the fading summer sun highlighted the clouds to the west. Emery had haphazardly packed a laundry bag half full, which he threw onto the far seat in the back of the buggy's cab. The seats must have been recently upholstered, for they smelled like new leather. Emery offered Ceony a hand into the buggy, and then climbed up after her.

"To Burleigh Road, if you would," Emery called to the driver. To Ceony, he said, "Stayed in a hotel there once. Decent place."

Ceony managed a smile. The buggy turned on its lights and circled around, plodding down the long road into London. Cooling summer air swept through the glassless windows and teased Emery's wavy hair. Shadowy trees whisked past them, thankfully shielding the river from view.

"I *am* sorry, Emery," Ceony said, resting her hands on her bag.

"It's hardly your fault," he said, and he lifted his left arm up and around her shoulders. Ceony's heart raced against its weight, and she dared not move for fear of scaring the gesture away. "If anything," he continued, "it's mine. If not for me, you wouldn't be involved in this business at all." He paused. "Actually, no. It's Patrice Aviosky's fault, for assigning you to me. Yes, let's blame her."

Ceony laughed and stifled a yawn. "I'm glad she did, though."

"You are certainly the most amusing apprentice I've had," Emery said in a strange sort of agreement. "Langston was the dullest."

"He's not much younger than you."

"No, he's not," Emery said. His thumb absently traced the edge of Ceony's braid, and Ceony thanked the darkness for hiding the reddening of her cheeks. "I was only twenty-four when I took him on, just two years out of my own apprenticeship. But the number of Folders had declined so rapidly that Praff was assigning to just about anyone. It was either me or sail across the ocean to New Orleans. Langston stayed in England to pursue a girl."

Clearing her throat and trying not to focus on Emery's closeness, Ceony asked, "Is he married now?"

Emery chuckled. "Goodness no. She wrote him quite the scathing letter two weeks into his apprenticeship. He was a bucket of sap for a month after that, but his focus improved in the end. Daniel, however, was a different story. He's the reason I moved to the cottage and started warding the gate."

Ceony let herself relax in her seat. Emery's arm remained around her shoulders. "Was he a troublemaker?"

"A flirt. An awful one at that, but somehow he attracted women who fell for his questionable charms," Emery said, thoughtful. "I had a new one on my doorstep every week, or so it seemed. That boy would have taken six years to earn his magicianship at the rate he was going. But another reason our time was cut short was the timing . . . and, well, you already know enough about that."

Ceony nodded, swallowing another yawn. She had only learned a snippet about Emery's second apprentice from her journey through Emery's heart; all she knew was that he had to be transferred because of issues with Lira.

Emery chuckled. "One girl who came by couldn't have been a day out of secondary. Tall as Langston. Daniel was a rather short fellow and seemed put out by her visit, but I invited her in, thinking maybe it would dissuade him from handing out my address like Halloween candy—"

A jolt in the road startled Ceony awake; she hadn't realized she'd dozed off, and perhaps Emery hadn't, either, for he was still chatting away beside her. Her head rested against his shoulder, and she straightened quickly, a new flush burning her skin.

"And it was shrimp," he said, shaking his head. "Who puts shrimp and sweet cream in the same dish? Certainly you've never heard of such a thing."

"It . . ." Ceony blinked sleep from her eyes. "It sounds like a soup I've seen in Devonshire," she said. "I don't think—"

She squinted through the windshield of the vehicle. Was that a person on the road, just beyond the glow of the buggy's lights?

The light fanned over him, and time stopped.

The man jerked his arm upward. The windshield didn't shatter and Ceony heard no pistol fire, but the driver's head jerked backward, spurting black blood over his seat and the windshield.

The driver slumped in his seat, falling against the steering wheel. The buggy's headlamps pulled away from the road, illuminating plants, earth, and finally—to Ceony's horror—the dark, churning water of the river. Emery gripped her shoulder, pressing his other hand against the ceiling to brace himself.

Time started again when the buggy hit the black water. Ceony jerked forward and grabbed the seat in front of her. Pain shot up her wrists. Darkness flooded the cab. Cold water pooled at her feet.

Snow-cold chills spread from Ceony's chest into her limbs, freezing her solid. Her thoughts shut down. Her heart stopped beating. Her throat went dry. Her legs turned numb.

"No no no no no no no no no!" she cried, but her voice sounded from somewhere else, somewhere distant. Water poured into the buggy, climbing like thousands of chilled spiders up her calves, knees, thighs—

Emery pushed against the door as water gushed in through the buggy's glassless window. The entire car slanted, its nose pushing for the river bottom.

Drowning. She was drowning. Tears poured down her cheeks, but she still couldn't move, not even as the water climbed up her legs and over the seat, up her blouse.

"I'm going to pull you out," Emery said, his words airy and quick.

"No no no . . . ," Ceony muttered, wide-eyed, clutching to the upholstery with white knuckles. "No no no no . . ."

Emery grabbed her arms, yanking them away from the driver's seat, and hooked them around his neck.

"Take a deep breath!" he shouted. "Hold on to me. Don't breathe again until we're out!"

The water climbed to her stomach, her breasts, her collar.

She started convulsing.

Emery cursed, inhaled deeply, and sealed his lips shut just as the water flooded above their chins, foreheads, crowns.

Ceony squeezed her eyes shut and dug her nails into Emery's neck, clinging to the fabric of his collar. She moved forward, jerked, and felt the top of the buggy window scrape against her back and thighs.

The next thing she knew, darkness engulfed her. Everything was cold save for Emery's neck and the burning in her lungs. She felt him kicking beside her, but the water . . . it didn't end. It didn't end!

And suddenly Ceony was seven years old again, falling into the Hendersons' fishpond, thrashing for the surface but only finding handfuls of mud and silt. *She couldn't breathe!*

And then the wetness broke and warm summer air touched her skin. Ceony sputtered and sucked in a hot breath, which scorched her throat like fire. She cleaved to Emery in the weightlessness of the water, like she was falling—

"Shhh, shhh," Emery urged her. One arm was wrapped tightly around her torso, pressing her to him, while the other swam back and forth, treading water. Then he stopped moving, and they began to sink. Ceony cried out, but the hand gripping her waist shot up and covered her mouth.

Emery kicked and they floated once more, only this time Emery held a small plastic case in his hand. He used his teeth to open it. Inside rested a Folded piece of paper.

He pinched it in his mouth, dropped the plastic case, and grabbed the paper with his wading arm. The water started to pull them under, but Emery whispered "Conceal" and threw the paper into the air. Ceony watched it unfurl in the starlight, expanding until it hovered over them like an umbrella a few feet above the water.

Emery continued to tread, inching toward the shore, the Conceal spell following them as they went. Conscious thoughts trickled back to Ceony bit by bit through the remnants of her panic. The buggy, the water. How had she gotten to the surface? Emery?

She squinted toward the road in the starlight, just barely able to see a silhouette there, at the edge of the bank. The man in the lights. She *had* seen a man.

Her feet hit muddy ground, and Emery stopped moving, his eyes glued to the figure he too had noticed.

A light appeared farther down the road—another buggy. For a brief moment it highlighted the tall, lanky form of the man standing there, his curly hair and dark skin. Ceony squinted, thinking she recognized him, but he vanished in a cloud of smoke before she could place him. The buggy lights slowed their approach, the driver perhaps perceiving the signs of the accident.

Both of Emery's arms embraced Ceony as the water surrounded them. "I'm sorry," he whispered into her wet hair. "I'm so sorry. It's all right now. You're all right."

He kissed her forehead.

Ceony came fully back to herself. She realized she was still crying, her tears scorching compared to the cold river water. Her teeth chattered.

Ceony buried her face in Emery's wet clothes, shivering, and stayed that way until a second set of buggy lights appeared on the road. Someone beamed a Gaffer light out onto the water.

"They're looking for us," Emery whispered. "Reveal," he said, and the spell hiding them folded itself back up and dropped into the water. Emery let the current carry it away. Then he helped Ceony up and guided her to the steep shore. She clung to him, not even loosening her grip when he waved one arm to the searchers, asking for help. One of them returned to his car, perhaps for rope, or another light.

"That wasn't Grath," Ceony murmured.

"No, it wasn't," Emery agreed.

Ceony detected familiarity in those words.

Whoever their attacker had been, Emery knew him.

CHAPTER 6

CEONY SAT IN A chair in the corner of the South London police station, thumbing the wet remnants of Fennel, who had been in her bag when the buggy hit the river. Emery had assured her that the dog could be repaired. At the moment, though, the paper magician was speaking to a local detective and Mg. Juliet Cantrell of Criminal Affairs behind a locked door, and Ceony sat alone in the empty police station, cradling the soggy remnants of her dog in her lap.

She stifled a yawn, and a hiccup, thanks to the small dose of cognac Mg. Cantrell had given her to calm her nerves. The cherry-wood cuckoo clock on the back wall struck thirty minutes past midnight.

Ceony turned her gaze to the door Emery had disappeared behind nearly an hour ago. He had been involved with law enforcement on a deeper level for years, Ceony knew, but she still wished she could hear the discussion. Emery had seemed rather adamant that she wait out here. Was he trying to protect her, or did he simply not trust her?

She had been as useful as a sack of weevil-eaten flour when the buggy went over the riverbank. Had she been alone, she would be dead in the water, floating alongside the driver, whose name she didn't even know.

The driver. The crash blurred in her memory, but she remembered his gruesome death clearly. A simple swipe of another's hand, and he had died. An Excision spell; Ceony had no other explanation for it.

The door opened. Ceony perked up, but only the detective emerged, holding an unmarked, yellow folder full of papers. From a glance, she could tell the folder had a "no-eyes" lock on it—it would only open when given a specific command, though that command did not necessarily need to come from a magician. Emery had taught her about that spell just last week.

The detective glanced around, set one paper on an unoccupied desk, and then crossed the room toward Ceony. He pulled up a chair and sat across from her, their knees just two feet apart. He held an expensive pen with a tiny Smelting seal on its end—a seal that would light up when the pen was about to run out of ink. Ceony had used similar pens during her schooling at Tagis Praff.

He set a ledger printed with the seal of Criminal Affairs on his lap.

Criminal Affairs, though strictly a branch of the Magicians' Cabinet, worked closely with all of England's law enforcement both domestically and abroad. A few magicians even worked with detective agencies that weren't associated with Criminal Affairs. Ceony assumed involvement with the Magicians' Cabinet got overly political, so she couldn't blame them.

Ceony took a long look at the detective before her, his coffee-stained shirt and what looked like a Smelted gun in a holster over his shoulder. Smelters often operated alongside law enforcement;

had Ceony become a Smelter like she'd originally planned, she might have been here under a different capacity.

The detective frowned. "Do you need a blanket, Miss Twill?"

Ceony shook her head, though her wet waistband had begun to itch. "I'm fine, thank you."

"I'm sorry to make you repeat yourself," the detective apologized, "but could you recount your story once more? Give me as many details as you can remember."

Chewing on her bottom lip, Ceony nodded. She recounted the accident as best she could, trying to keep her voice smooth, though that proved difficult when she spoke of the driver's fate. She couldn't recount more than the beginning and the end of the story—once the buggy hit the water, her mind had just stopped working.

Useless.

The detective asked her a few more questions, then thanked her and stood, returning his chair to the desk he had borrowed it from. A few moments later, he disappeared back into the closed room where Mg. Cantrell and Emery were still talking.

The front door to the police station opened, and in walked Mg. Aviosky, a very exhausted-looking Delilah, and Mg. Hughes, a Siper—rubber magician—whom Ceony had formally met after Emery's brush with death three months ago. Mg. Hughes sat on the Magicians' Cabinet for Criminal Affairs, and Ceony knew from the third chamber of Emery's heart that he was the one who'd involved Emery in hunting Excisioners in the first place.

Ceony stood and set Fennel and the rest of her soaked belongings down on her chair.

Mg. Aviosky reached her first and seized her shoulders, taking a moment to look her up and down. "You have a knack for getting into danger, Miss Twill," she said with a click of her tongue, followed by a sigh of relief. "Thank goodness you're well." Her face paled. "Magician Thane?"

"He's fine, just a bump on his head," Ceony said. She hadn't noticed the injury—and the dried blood coming down from Emery's hairline—until they had reached the police station.

She was completely and utterly useless.

"He's talking with Magician Cantrell," she finished, gesturing to the closed door across the room. She had met Mg. Cantrell—a Smelter—only briefly. She had seemed far more interested in Emery's account of the accident than in Ceony's.

Delilah pushed forward and gave Ceony a tight hug, but spared her the double kiss. "Oh, Ceony, I'm so sorry. How dreadful this must be."

"I'm all right," Ceony said, though she felt less than confident in her answer. She felt tired, frightened, worried, relieved, anxious—did "all right" fit with any of those?

"You've filed your reports?" Mg. Hughes asked. He sounded gruffer than Ceony remembered, but that could have been due to the late hour.

She nodded.

Mg. Hughes frowned and rubbed his trimmed white beard with his thumb and forefinger. "A knack for danger is something of an understatement. This is the third incident you've been involved in this week."

"Third?" Mg. Aviosky repeated, eyes bugging behind her thin glasses.

Mg. Hughes nodded. "I received a report yesterday evening concerning the reappearance of Grath Cobalt. Seems he's back in town, and he paid Miss Twill a personal visit."

Delilah gripped Ceony's arm to her chest and shuddered.

Mg. Aviosky's skin paled. "But he left England!"

"So we thought," Mg. Hughes said. "But he's come back for this one."

"No, he's come back for Lira," Ceony interjected, adjusting her damp shirt with her free arm. The towel she had been given upon her arrival had already soaked through and now hung off the back of her chair. "He thinks I have the secret to restoring her."

But Ceony barely understood how she defeated Lira in the first place. They had fought outside the cave. In a struggle for Lira's knife, Ceony had sliced open the woman's eye . . . and in a moment that her memory could still not piece together, Ceony had written *Lira froze* on a piece of damp paper. Written as she would a story illusion. Only Lira's frozen state was no illusion.

"Seems he didn't like your response," Mg. Hughes said, intrigued.

"No," said a tired baritone behind them—Ceony recognized the voice as Emery's. "This wasn't Grath."

They all turned toward Emery. Mg. Cantrell, who had also emerged from the office, was busily writing something in a ledger at a nearby desk. Delilah's grip on Ceony's arm tightened even more.

"Ceony agrees with me on that much," Emery said, giving Ceony a sympathetic look. She felt a surge of relief that the paper magician wasn't angry with her for making a bad situation worse— or, at least, he didn't seem to be. "I don't know for sure. I had a poor vantage point and it was dark, but I suspect that Saraj Prendi might still be in cahoots with Grath."

Mg. Hughes frowned. "We haven't heard high or low on Prendi for nearly three years."

"I imagine you have," Emery said, "you just didn't know it was him."

Mg. Hughes scoffed, but he didn't debate the point.

"Who is Saraj?" asked Delilah.

Mg. Hughes sighed. "Perhaps you should take your apprentice to another room, Patrice."

"Please let her stay," Ceony said. "She should know, too. She was almost part of it."

Delilah's mouth dropped, but she kept her wits about her enough not to ask how for the time being.

Mg. Aviosky nodded, and Mg. Hughes shrugged.

"Saraj Prendi is an Excisioner who hails from India," the Siper said. "At least, his lineage is Indian. We don't have enough details on his history to confirm his place of birth. But we do have a solid criminal profile on him."

Gooseflesh prickled Ceony's arms.

"Which is?" Mg. Aviosky asked.

"He's unpredictable," Mg. Hughes said. "Sometimes he does solo jobs; sometimes he works with large groups of Excisioners, such as the one Grath Cobalt used to lead, until our sting operation in 1901 disbanded it. Two things we *do* know are that Saraj Prendi likes to show off, and he has a distinct lack of conscience."

"Show off," Ceony said, "like with explosions."

"Perhaps," Mg. Hughes said, "but we have no evidence to link him to the paper mill. In fact, we have nothing to tie the mill to these other events save for *you*, Miss Twill."

Ceony thought of the Indian man she had seen in the crowd outside the mill after the explosion, thought of the strange feeling of being watched that had prickled her skin that day. She shuddered.

"I think it was him," she whispered. "I think . . . I think I saw him, outside the mill. Dark skin, dark eyes . . . thin, with a half beard, right? I think he was there."

Emery's brows drew together, making his forehead crease. His eyes glimmered in a way that reminded Ceony of the heat that rose from sunbaked cobblestone streets.

Ceony's body itched under her clothes. What if Saraj had gotten close enough to touch her? What if one simple gesture on that road had sent her blood flying, too?

"Well," Mg. Hughes said, sounding quite sober, "if that's the case—"

Ceony shook her head hard enough that Delilah, who was still clinging to her, stumbled. "But they can't be working together! Grath wanted me to *cooperate* with him. He wants to hear what happened at Foulness Island from my lips. If he kills me, he won't get his answers. Even if this other man *is* Saraj Prendi, he couldn't possibly be working with Grath. Grath wants me alive, and I think it's fairly obvious that Saraj does not."

"Very astute," Emery commented darkly.

Mg. Aviosky nodded. "A good point, if an uneasy one."

Mg. Hughes returned to rubbing his beard. "And yet they both seem fixated on Ceony. I can think of no motivation for Saraj outside of Grath's direction, unless they've become cross with one another. But if I recall correctly"—he glanced to Emery—"Saraj greatly disliked Lira. I highly doubt her well-being would be any motivating factor of his."

Emery nodded.

"So, if they are working together," Mg. Hughes said, "they have different agendas. Methinks there's a great deal of miscommunication going on between our suspects."

"And a great deal of speculation is going on in this room," Emery said, pushing between Mg. Hughes and Mg. Aviosky to reach Ceony. He rested a hand on her shoulder, which immediately earned him a frown from Mg. Aviosky. "And this is all the speculation we can manage for one night. Ceony and I need to find somewhere to stay in the city until this can be sorted out."

"I've already made arrangements," Mg. Aviosky said, though that frown still tugged on the corners of her lips, as though a string tied her mouth directly to Emery's resting fingers. "There's a flat not far from my home that you can lease for the time being. It's in a well-populated area. I have a driver waiting to take you there."

"Thank you," Emery said. "I appreciate it."

Mg. Hughes stayed behind to discuss Mg. Cantrell's findings while Ceony and Emery followed Mg. Aviosky and Delilah out to the street, which was illuminated by tall lamps glowing with enchanted fire encased in glass that wouldn't snuff it out. Mg. Aviosky's buggy seated eight and had glass that covered every window. Mg. Aviosky used a spell to tint the back windows black, concealing the automobile's passengers in the dark of night.

Big Ben chimed one in the morning when the automobile pulled up to a twelve-story brick building four blocks from Parliament Square. Ceony and Emery's temporary flat was located on the top floor, and it consisted of a long living room, a large bedroom, a narrow kitchen and vanity room, and a bathroom.

Emery headed straight for the sofa in the living room. His footsteps reverberated along the wooden flooring until he stepped onto an old country rug, which muted the sound.

"Ceony," Mg. Aviosky said before Ceony could step through the doorway. Delilah remained outside in the car, leaving Ceony and her former mentor alone. "I think it would be best for you to go abroad for the time being, since these incidents seem to center around you. I know a paper magician in Kingsland, Wales, who could take you on, so as to minimize the interruption—"

"No!" Ceony said, a bit too quickly. "I'd like to stay with Emery. Magician Thane, I mean."

Mg. Aviosky's eyebrows knit together, and Ceony cursed herself for using Emery's first name in front of her. An apprentice *never* called a magician by his or her first name. Such a thing wasn't proper.

"I mean, I think it would be a greater hindrance for everyone involved for me to try and move now," Ceony amended. "If I have the option, I would prefer to stay in London."

Mg. Aviosky's look of disapproval was unmistakable. A curt nod made Ceony's stomach clench.

"Take care of yourself, Miss Twill," Mg. Aviosky said, stepping back into the hallway. "I'll be checking in on you soon."

Sunlight from the wide square window near the bed woke Ceony, and despite the late hour at which she had turned in for the night, she couldn't coax her body to sleep more. Too many thoughts ran through her mind. Why would another Excisioner want to hurt her? Where was Grath, and what would his next move be? How long would this new flat be safe?

And what did Mg. Aviosky think of her? And Emery?

She pulled herself from bed, wearing only her under-things and a chemise. She never slept so scandalously, especially with a man in the adjoining room, but all her clothes had been soaked last night, so her choice had been between sleeping in damp under-things or nothing at all, which would have been especially humiliating had she needed to vacate the room quickly.

She flushed, the pinkness visible on her chest and arms, and hurried to her closet, where she had hung her clothes to dry. The second set she had packed seemed wearable. The first would need to be washed, as they bore mud stains from the riverbank and had dried stiff.

She changed with haste and brushed out her hair, but didn't bother with makeup. Not today. She didn't think kohl and rouge would do her any good, and her cosmetics probably needed to dry out, too.

When she opened the bedroom door, she found the living room bathed in bright sunlight, thanks to its east-facing window. The lavender sofa was empty save for a folded blanket perfectly aligned with the rightmost cushion. Emery sat at a tall, walnut-stained desk against the wall. He had hung his indigo coat by the door and wore the simple white button-up shirt and gray slacks he had donned the day before.

He Folded Fennel's front left leg.

"Emery!" Ceony exclaimed, running to him. He had a stack of clean, white paper—where had he gotten that?—next to him, as well as Fennel, almost fully formed now. The paper forming his ears and part of his torso was slightly wrinkled, damaged from the river.

"When did you have time to do this?" she asked, ogling his handiwork and the circles under his eyes. "You never went to bed. You pretended to go to bed and did this instead!"

Emery smiled. "I had a lot to think about. I didn't mind."

"You're insufferable," she mumbled, tears burning the corners of her eyes. She touched Fennel's new muzzle, splayed sideways on the desk. A little more work and he would be able to reanimate. "You need to rest," she added, a little quieter.

Emery leaned back in his chair and stretched his arms out in a wide V. "A nap *would* be nice. What time is it?"

Ceony frowned. Had Emery really suffered a bout of insomnia, or had he done this for her?

"It's seven thirty," she said. "Thank you. It means a lot to me."

His eyes smiled at her.

"I'll make you breakfast," Ceony declared, taking one step toward the kitchen. She paused. "We have no food."

Emery rubbed his chin. "I believe you are correct, unless Patrice took time to stock the cupboards before we arrived. Given the short notice, I consider that highly unlikely."

He glanced back to his work. "Give me a few more minutes here and we can pick up some provisions."

Ceony reached for his face—watching those tired eyes—but retracted her hand, thinking better of it. She remembered again the look Mg. Aviosky had given her.

"You should rest first," she said instead.

"I'd rather not," Emery confessed. "I'd like to stay alert. And hidden, but I know of no businesses that deliver groceries, and while

I saw a telegraph in the lobby downstairs, I wouldn't know how to contact them, besides."

Ceony excused herself to write up a grocery list, which included soap for their filthy clothes. She stashed extra paper in her bag in case of an emergency and left the room. Emery had finished Fennel, but he left him unanimated on the desk. He pulled on his indigo coat and led the way out the door. Other early risers sparsely dusted the street outside.

"I suppose we should go to the west end of Parliament Square for these things," Emery said as he looked over Ceony's list. "It's always crowded there, which will be to our benefit."

He sighed and handed the list back to Ceony. "What a bother. This place is like a bad cold."

"Congested and tiring?"

Emery's eyes shimmered with amusement. "Precisely. I like how you think, Ceony."

Ceony permitted herself to bask in the compliment for as long as it took them to reach the market, which, thanks to the location of the complex where they were staying, was only about ten minutes away. Long lines of vendors sold goods from stands clustered at the far west end of Parliament Square, most of them local farmers. The stands formed two narrow streets, which were already crowded with customers weighing tomatoes and holding beaded jewelry up to the spare sunlight. A few pigeons had gathered at the corners of the market to peck for crumbs, and Big Ben chimed the hour behind them.

As Ceony examined a small wheel of cheese at a dairy stand painted bright green, she said, "I *am* expecting an extension on my homework in light of everything."

"Absolutely not."

Ceony put the cheese in her cloth bag while Emery paid the vendor. "Why not?"

"Magicians must constantly work under pressure," Emery said matter-of-factly, "and so must you. *Perhaps* one more attempt on your life will make me reconsider, but until then, lessons and assignments will proceed as normal." He paused. "Though I suspect you left the paper doll behind, hmm? I'll think of some other sort of busywork."

Ceony frowned.

She approached a wide vegetable stand draped in a turquoise cloth edged with bobbin lace. A few departing patrons bumped into her as she squeezed by; the narrow street in combination with the narrow storefronts offered little in the way of personal space. Despite herself, her stomach churned uneasily, as if it were full of cream that couldn't quite make itself into butter. She picked up a red bell pepper and examined it without really seeing it.

When Emery came closer, she said, "I really am sorry about last night. I understand if you're upset."

He glanced at her, genuine surprise in his emerald irises. "You're hardly the one who crashed the car, Ceony," he said in a low voice.

Ceony set the pepper down. "I know. It's not that, I just . . ."

She released a long breath and stepped back from the stand, moving away from the bulk of the crowd. "It's just that I was about as useful as that half-cut paper doll in my bedroom. I know you expect more of me."

Emery nodded, though his eyes looked sympathetic. Ceony waited for a moment before moving on to the next stand, where she grabbed a small bundle of carrots and some thyme.

Once they returned to the center of the road, having navigated around two men who'd had the audacity to bring their horses into the crowded market, Emery said, "I understand why you'd think that, Ceony, but I don't hold any malice toward you. Certainly you know that."

She just nodded.

"We all have our fears," he said, placing a hand on her back to guide her around a gaggle of gossiping women. His touch felt light, but warm, and welcome. "You understand mine; it's only fair that I try and understand yours."

She glanced back at him, surprised. "I . . . thank you."

He rubbed his eyes, which had finally grown heavy with fatigue. "Let's see . . . list. Rhubarb is over here, I think."

"Rhubarb isn't on the—"

"And we'll need flour if you're making that pie tonight," he continued, pointing to a wide stand showcasing various types of produce. Ceony had thought the season for rhubarb was over, but these farmers had some of the red stalks in their wares.

She smiled. "In that case, I'll also need eggs and butter. I only brought one bag, but I'm sure there's space in that coat of yours."

"The gray one has more pockets."

Ceony selected a few stalks of rhubarb, wondering if the kitchen in their temporary home was stocked with any pie tins, when a familiar, uneasy feeling settled over her skin—the same prickling sensation she'd experienced at the paper mill in Dartford.

She froze for a moment, but Emery's hand found her back again, and he pushed her farther down the road.

"Look ahead," he murmured. "I believe we're being followed. Let's loop around to check, hmm?"

The hair on Ceony's arms stood on end, but she nodded and focused on looking straight ahead. Her pulse quickened, pushing against her neck, and she couldn't tell whether it was from fear or Emery's fingers pressing into her shoulder blades. She groaned inwardly. How enamored could one woman be?

They turned left through the stands, passing tables of beads and leather goods, and then moved back behind the produce sellers until they once again reached the man with the red peppers. Ceony picked up the closest one to purchase, hoping to make their movements look as natural as possible. Emery flowed right with the act, paying the seller and thanking him for his trouble.

They began walking again, weaving through other customers. Emery reached into his coat and pulled out a roll of paper, which he began to roll even tighter around his pinky finger.

Before long, he had formed a paper telescope.

Ceony glanced at his sleeves. "How much stuff do you keep in there?"

Emery just smiled, then pulled Ceony behind a used-book shop. Peering around the corner of the building, Emery extended the telescope's length and said, "Zoom." He searched the street for a few long seconds before shortening the telescope and returning it to his coat.

"Quite the bold man, that one."

"Grath?" Ceony asked. She wondered how badly he had been burned by her Burst spell.

"No, Saraj. At least, I think that's him. He's wearing a hood, and he's alone."

"Let me see."

Emery hesitated.

She held out her hand, waiting, and the paper magician reluctantly handed her the telescope, which still held its Magnification spell. It took Ceony a moment, but then her telescope landed on a fairly tall man—shorter than Grath, she supposed—a ways down the road, wearing a jacket much too warm for the climate, its unfashionable hood pulled up and over his face. It could have been the shadows, but he resembled the man she had seen near the mill and after the buggy accident. She couldn't get a clear look at his face, however.

Ceony lowered the telescope and ducked back around the corner of the bookstore. Her skin prickled even more—perhaps that was the body's natural reaction to an Excisioner's gaze.

Emery took the telescope back from her. "I want you to circle around this shop and head toward the bank. Don't stop for anything. Go to the flat's back entrance, understand?"

Tingles like electricity ran up Ceony's sides and into her skull. She grabbed Emery's forearm. "Please don't," she whispered, pleaded. "Please, please don't go after him now. I don't want you to get hurt."

"I know what I'm doing," Emery said.

And that's why you haven't caught him yet, because you know what you're doing? Ceony wanted to say, but she kept the thought to herself.

Another phrase came to mind. "Let me come with you."

He frowned. "Absolutely not."

"Don't you trust me?"

Fine lines creased Emery's brow. He glanced back around the bookstore before saying, "This is not a matter of trust."

Isn't it? But Ceony knew when she couldn't win an argument. Instead, she tried another tack.

"I'll be left alone," she said. A pregnant woman passed them, and Ceony held her tongue until the woman was out of earshot. "And I'm the one's he's after, right?"

Emery pressed his lips into a thin line. He glanced back around the corner of the bookstore—only a glance—and nodded. "All right. We'll take a long route home, however. Find a place where we can telegraph his location to the police. I don't want him spying any of my spells."

Ceony nodded and forced herself to release her crab-claw grip on Emery's forearm. She must have been squeezing harder than she realized, because Emery rubbed the spot when she released him.

They took a very, very long route home, so long that Ceony's feet and hips hurt by the time they reached the complex.

Ceony couldn't help but feel like they'd been walking on egg-shells.

CHAPTER 7

CEONY MADE A SIMPLE stew for dinner that night, cooking and seasoning with care to make it taste as good as she could manage with their limited supplies. Mg. Aviosky had stopped by earlier to bring them some extra groceries, as well as some ledgers from Mg. Hughes for Emery. Emery had been absorbed in the books ever since.

He ate at the desk, and Ceony took her own supper into the bedroom, where Fennel yipped until she let him smell the bowl. Being made of paper, Fennel couldn't eat the stew, but Emery had crafted him with the doglike mannerisms anyway. For a man allergic to canines, he certainly knew them well.

Ceony read to the thirteenth chapter in her origami textbook, storing the words to memory as she went, rereading important passages or anything Emery had highlighted to ensure the knowledge stuck. She fingered the barrette in her hair—the one Emery had made her—as she studied. She hoped they would return to the cottage soon. She had grown rather fond of the place, cluttered though it was. Nothing spectacular had happened after the trip to the market that morning, so perhaps they would head back soon. Ceony knew it wouldn't happen, not until there was some resolution to this situation, but she could hope, at least.

She washed her clothes and Emery's, using a Fan spell to help dry them, then bathed and got ready for bed. She peeked out the closed curtains over her bedroom window before settling in for the night. The city lights provided only scant illumination, however, and the night hid the street from her, save for the occasional passing of a buggy's headlamps smearing over the cobblestones like butter over hot bread.

Ceony sighed. She hated being stuck like this, waiting for enemies to make their moves. At least with Lira she had been able to take matters into her own hands, more or less. Even trapped inside Emery's heart, she could always move forward, make progress. Here, the tall buildings and clustered streets of the city had her trapped like a mouse in a maze, without even the possible reward of cheese. Perhaps that was why Emery hated the city so much.

She turned off her lamp, but noticed dim light streaming in from under her door. She went to the living room, where Emery sat on the end of the couch, reading over yet another ledger.

She watched him a moment, his focus, the slouch to his shoulders, the way the electric light gleamed off the waves of his hair. She had thought Magician Emery Thane very common looking, once. How silly she had been.

A minute passed before Emery sensed her and looked up from his work.

"You'll turn to mush if you don't get some rest," Ceony warned, spying his dinner bowl on the desk. She crossed the room to fetch it; how unlike him to be untidy, even on this small a scale. Those ledgers had to be incredibly absorbing. And that worried her.

"I'll turn in soon," he said.

"Hmm," Ceony hummed, doubting him. She'd have to start drugging him with poppy seeds and chamomile just to get him on a half-normal sleep schedule. What *would* the man do without an apprentice to look after him?

She headed for the kitchen, but Emery stopped her. "Ceony," he said.

She glanced back. Emery remained on the couch, but he'd extended his left hand to her.

Ceony assumed he wanted his bowl back, for whatever reason, but when she held it out to him, he reached past the dish to her wrist and gently tugged her onto the couch beside him.

Shivers ran over her skin like hundreds of ants. Ceony opened her mouth in question, but Emery merely put his arm around her shoulders and continued to read his ledger, the pages of which had been crammed margin to margin with tiny, cramped handwriting not nearly as refined as his own.

The shivers fled, and just like they always did when he was near, her cheeks and chest blushed at his closeness. After a moment she permitted herself to relax. Sitting against him, and without the indigo coat between them, it surprised Ceony how warm Emery felt, like a campfire crackled beneath his skin. Not feverishly warm, just . . . comfortable.

She laid her head against him as she had in the car, and his fingers curled around her shoulder. Her pulse raced, and she could hear his heart through his shoulder. It was beating steadily, but perhaps a bit more quickly than normal. After all, she knew Emery's heartbeat almost as well as her own.

He smelled like soap and brown sugar. She glanced up at the stubble beginning to grow on his face, heavier close to his long sideburns and finer as it neared his lips. She studied his lips for a moment, their shape, their smoothness. She dropped her gaze before she could flush too deeply.

Her pulse gradually slowed as she let herself absorb the moment, the perfectness of it all, until her thoughts lulled her into warm, equally perfect dreams.

———

Ceony awoke the next morning to Fennel tugging on her messy braid. She stared at her surroundings—the desk, the ceiling, the window—in confusion for a moment before registering where she lay. The flat in the city: the living room. She lay on her side on the sofa, her legs curled up and her right foot asleep. A tan blanket was draped over her.

She bolted up, knocking Fennel to the floor. The dog yapped in protest, but shook his head and took to sniffing about the baseboards.

Ceony saw no sign of Emery, but there was a piece of paper bearing his beautiful script on the chair of the desk, which had been turned to face her.

Blinking sleep from her eyes, she read:

> I've gone to Magician Hughes's home in Lambeth (47 Wickham Street) to discuss some matters of importance. I've warded the flat, so I beg you to stay inside its confines until I return. I've left a Mimic spell as well, in case you need to contact me.

Ceony lowered the note and looked at the desk. Sure enough, there was a torn piece of paper with the word "Mimic" written across the top of it.

> I should only be a couple of hours, and Patrice is close by in case of an emergency.
>
> In the meantime, you'll find some paper in the desk's top drawer and instructions for making a shrinking chain (inanimate objects only,

I'm afraid). I'd like to see twenty-one links completed when I return. Threats on your well-being are poor excuses for missing homework!

He drew a happy face after that—two dots and a curving line—and signed his name.

Ceony sighed and set the note down, then retrieved the instructions for the shrinking chain. While Emery had flawless penmanship and could form perfect Folds with his eyes closed, those were the extent of his artistic abilities. Ceony turned his sloppy diagrams of the steps for making the chain this way and that, trying to make sense of them. She had a fair idea how to make and connect the links, but she would have to fiddle with them herself to determine if she had interpreted the instructions correctly.

Locating a charcoal pencil, she wrote on the Mimic spell, *And surely you don't mind my practicing on your things, correct?*

Avoid using my clothing, please, he replied.

She set the pencil down and adjourned to the kitchen for some oatmeal. She washed the dishes—what few they had—and changed into her now clean first set of clothing. She organized her things in the bedroom, folded the blanket on the couch, and folded a paper cube for Fennel to fetch before finally sitting down for her assignment.

It took her four tries to correctly Fold the first link of the shrinking chain, which frustrated her greatly, as Ceony was not used to doing something wrong more than once. Each link was made of two pieces of 4" by 5½" paper, which Folded together into a hook of sorts. Ceony had begun Folding the third link when she heard something tapping in the next room.

She glanced up. "Fennel?" she called.

But the paper dog sat licking his paws at the foot of the couch.

Ceony hesitated, a half-formed link in her hand, but she heard the tapping again, like a fingernail against a window: tap tap tap tap.

She stood from her chair, listening. It hadn't come from the window.

Ceony wandered into the kitchen, and the noise rang out a third time, louder: tap tap tap tap. The vanity room.

She opened the door. The only light in the room came from a high window concealed by sheer curtains that made the air look blue. The space was fairly empty, save for a closet, a makeup stand and chair, and an antique full-length mirror in the far corner.

And in that mirror, Ceony saw the face of Grath Cobalt.

Gasping, she spun around, expecting the Excisioner to be standing behind her. No one was there.

"Looks like I got the right place," he said from the mirror, his voice carrying a slight, ringing echo to it.

Ceony whirled back to the mirror, wide-eyed. Her ribs trembled with each beat of her very alert heart.

"You," she said, eyes darting about the room. But he wasn't there. He could only be seen in the mirror. She narrowed her eyes and dared to take a step closer. Grath grinned at her from the mirror's smooth surface, his left cheek still burned from her Burst spell.

Calm, she told herself. Then, aloud, "How did you find me?"

Grath opened his hands and let his fingers flutter. "Magic," he said. "Mirrors are eyes to anyone who knows how to use them."

He held up the ornate makeup mirror Delilah had given her at the bistro. She had left it behind in her purse when she fled the restaurant. Had he somehow used it to find her?

Ceony didn't respond; she folded her hands behind her back to hide their shaking. Staring into the mirror, past Grath, she studied his surroundings. There was an old, unpainted armoire, white blinds drawn over a sunny window, and the corner of a bed. If it was a hotel, it wasn't a very nice one. Somewhere with an east-facing window. A Gaffer must be standing somewhere out of Ceony's line of sight, for only a glass magician could enchant the mirrors Grath had used to reach her.

"Where are you?" she asked.

Grath laughed, then turned toward the bed, briefly revealing the unmarked door to his room. His image faltered for a moment as he mumbled something, then it expanded, revealing his body down to midthigh. He shut the makeup mirror in his hand and tossed it onto the bed.

The room seemed small, and Ceony hadn't spied another magician. Wherever the Gaffer was hiding, Grath hadn't given him orders to make a transfer to this larger mirror he now used.

"We never got to finish our conversation," Grath said, his lips pulling back to reveal that feline smile. "You were about to explain a spell to me."

Ceony's heart pulsed in her throat. Her feet grew cold. Could Grath possibly be . . . but how? It was only possible for a magician to bond with one material.

"It's you," she whispered.

Grath raised an eyebrow. "Excuse me?"

"Mirrors are eyes to anyone who knows how to use them," Ceony repeated, her stomach swirling. "You're . . . you're not an Excisioner. You're a Gaffer."

Grath laughed, a hearty sound that would have shattered his mirror had it been just a little louder. "How astute of you," he said. "Our little secret, hmm? A mistake I made a long time ago. But I want to remedy it, Ceony. In fact, I'm hoping the little spell you used on Lira might open a new window for me, if you'll excuse the pun."

"A window for what?" Ceony asked, sharpness leaking into her voice. "You can't bond to blood, and I certainly won't help you! Do you even care about Lira, or is power your only motivation?"

Grath scowled and stepped close enough to the mirror that his breath fogged the glass. "The first thing I'll do with you when this is over is rip those flapping lips off your face, Folder. Lira and I had plans. We were going to get away from you and your self-righteous system, but you couldn't let that happen, could you? I'm going to break whatever curse you put on her, and I'm going to make you my first test rat once blood is my domain."

Test rat? Ceony stepped back from the mirror, standing just off-center of the room. "You're serious," she breathed, but she didn't refer to the threats. Grath really *did* intend to break his bond to glass. But such a thing was impossible! Once a person formed a bond with a material, it couldn't be undone. The oath said as much!

"Tell me what you did to her!" Grath shouted, his thick fingers clutching the edge of the mirror. "Tell me what strange magic you have, this spell that bridges materials!"

"Even if I could free Lira, I'd let you flay me before I let the secret slip!" she shouted.

A creaking sound to her right startled Ceony. When she glanced to the side, she spied Emery's silhouette in the doorway, just out of sight of the mirror.

Grath didn't seem to notice. "I can make you break that promise," he said.

I have to keep him talking, Ceony thought, but before she could ask her next question, her mirror began to ripple, as though the glass was morphing into water.

Water . . . people could pass through water.

"Ceony!" Emery shouted. He threw open the door and pulled a Folded piece of paper from his long coat, but Ceony moved faster. She grabbed the chair by the makeup stand and flung it into the mirror, shattering it into hundreds of pieces. The glass rained over the floor, unmoving and solid. The pieces reflected only the ceiling and Ceony's huffing shoulders.

Grath had vanished.

Emery lowered his spell, palmed it. "A blind box, quickly."

Ceony pushed past him and into the living room. She ran to the desk, pulling four sheets of paper from its drawer. She Folded them, her flying fingers barely registering the tingling of the material. Emery had taught her the Blind Box spell two months after her arrival—a simple box that shut out everything beyond its paper walls, including light. Ceony had thought it fairly useless at the time, but it would prove efficient in nullifying Grath's spell if he still held any control over the mirror's shards.

She made four of them and hurried back to the vanity room.

Emery stood rigid, watching the shards. Ceony dropped down beside him and began to pick them up and shove them into the boxes. Emery crouched and helped her. One of the shards left a thin cut across her thumb, but she ignored it. Once they'd collected all the pieces, they shut the boxes' lids and left them sitting on the carpet.

"Seven years," Ceony said, catching her breath. "That's seven years' bad luck, you know."

Emery sniffed. "I think Lady Luck will grant you a pardon in this case."

"How much did you hear?"

"Enough," he said. He coughed softly and said, "Grath Cobalt . . . a Gaffer. A few things make sense now. Strange. Hughes will want to know." His voice sounded hoarse.

"Will he find us?" Ceony asked, staring at the boxes. Her fingers danced around their corners, checking her Folds for accuracy.

"No," Emery said, and he coughed. "He shouldn't know where we are, physically, if I understand mirror-hopping correctly. At least, I hope that's the case."

Ceony looked directly at the paper magician, finally noticing the redness of his eyes and puffiness around his jaw. He sniffed again, and barely any air made it through his sinuses.

"Goodness, Emery!" she exclaimed, standing. "What happened to you?"

Emery cleared his throat, but the action resulted in a fit of low coughs. Once he recovered, he grumbled, "Mrs. Hughes is a great lover of cats; unfortunately, this was unclear to me until I had already been exposed."

He coughed again and covered his mouth, which is when Ceony noticed the hives on his hand.

Ceony's own hand flew to her chest. "Magician Aviosky wasn't joking when she said you had allergies. Oh, Emery, you look awful."

"Thank you," he wheezed.

Clucking her tongue, Ceony took him by the sleeve and led him into the living room, where she half-shoved him onto the sofa and ordered him to lie down. He looked even worse in the better lighting; a few pink hives dotted his neck, and angry red zigzags marred the whites of his eyes.

"We have," he coughed, "a more important matter to deal with, Ceony."

Unfurling the folded blanket, Ceony said, "And I will deal with it. I can send a bird, and there's a telegraph downstairs. Grath isn't going anywhere, and neither are you. My brother is allergic to alfalfa, and whenever he gets sick we have to treat it like a cold. He doesn't get as sick as you are, though."

Emery responded with a heavy cough.

Frowning, Ceony let the blanket fall over him and ordered him to remove his coat, which was doubtlessly covered in cat hair, then hurried into the kitchen to fill two glasses with water. She pulled the desk chair over to the couch and set the glasses on top of it.

"Drink both of these. It will help flush you out," she instructed.

"I'm perfectly capable—" Emery began, but a wet and unpleasant cough cut off his words. Giving up, he reached for the first glass and downed it in five gulps.

Ceony returned to the kitchen and heated the stove to boil water—she didn't have a chicken, but she could make him some vegetable broth, which had never hurt anyone. She glanced back into the living room, where Emery was gulping down his second glass of water. His neck looked even more swollen.

Ceony felt her blood drain to her feet. "Do I need to call an ambulance?" she asked. "Have you had to go to the hospital before?"

Emery shook his head. "Only as a," he coughed, sniffed, "child. This will pass."

Ceony chewed on her lip and stepped back into the kitchen. After searching all the drawers, most of which were empty, she found a thin dish towel and soaked it in cool water. Returning to the living room, she used couch cushions to prop up Emery's head and wrapped the cool cloth just below his jaw, hoping it would alleviate the swelling. She then went to work at the desk, Folding and cutting snowflakes—a lesson she had learned in her first week as an apprentice.

The word "snow" enchanted them, but she gave them no direction for a falling pattern. Instead, she tucked them under the wet towel to keep it cool, then began braiding two paper bandages—the only solution she could think of for the hives.

She had learned how to make the bandages during the second month of her apprenticeship after accidentally walking in on Emery in the privy while he was trimming his hair over the sink. Her embarrassment at seeing the privy occupied, as well as seeing Emery shirtless, had startled her so greatly that she hadn't taken the time to remove her fingers from the doorframe before slamming the door closed, all while shouting a profuse apology. She had nearly broken her right middle finger in the process, and Emery had crafted one of these bandages to hasten its healing.

She finished crafting the bandages and wrapped one around each of Emery's hands, braiding the ends so they fit snugly. She then hurried down the switchback stairs rather than waiting for the lift, Emery's protests bouncing off her back as she went. When she reached the long, olive-and-tan-tiled lobby, she hurried past a clay urn and a tall mirror to reach the receptionist's desk. Ceony asked to use the telegraph and, after checking to ensure the woman was looking away, telegraphed Mg. Aviosky. She didn't know how to reach Mg. Hughes.

grath contacted through mirror stop he is a gaffer stop alert hughes and contact us stop

That message would raise more questions than it would answer, but Ceony imagined Mg. Aviosky would arrive at the apartment by nightfall. Ceony could explain the situation more fully in person.

After taking the lift back upstairs, Ceony busied herself with preparations for the broth. It took about an hour, and for at least half that time Emery coughed and sniffled. His feline-induced ailment had settled down somewhat by the time Ceony brought the steaming bowl of soup to his bedside.

She set it on the chair and sat on the edge of the lavender couch, pressing a hand to Emery's forehead.

"At least you don't have a fever," she said. "Well, I don't think you do. I'd rather not test you the way my mother taught me."

Emery laughed, some mirth shining through his red-veined eyes.

"You didn't *pet* the cats, did you?" she asked.

Emery cleared his throat, twice. "Heavens no. I only spied one of them on my way out. By then I knew I was a dead man. I thought I had come down with a cold, at first."

"How many does she own?"

"Four."

"I think that's two cats too many for anyone," Ceony said. She sighed, then gestured to the bowl. "Drink this when you're ready, but don't wait too long. And I'll get you more water."

She refilled the glasses in the kitchen and set them beside the broth.

Emery watched her as she reclaimed her seat on the edge of the couch, by his hip. After a moment, he asked, "Why do you do all of this for me, Ceony?"

A flush crept into her ears. She leaned away and stirred the broth. "Don't ask me that," she replied, quiet. She watched little bits of carrot and potato churn in the soup. She took a deep breath, then another, waiting for the flush to recede. When she was confident that it had, she said, "You know why."

"Ceony . . ." Emery's voice trailed off, but he didn't complete the thought, if he had intended to say anything more than her name to begin with. Ceony continued to stir the broth, which gave her something to focus on other than him.

A full minute passed before Emery spoke again.

He began with a sigh. "You're my apprentice. I don't . . . don't think I need to remind you of that."

"There's no documented rule against it," Ceony countered. The flush began to creep across her skin again, betraying her. "I checked."

Emery rubbed under the wet cloth around his neck. He hesitated, perhaps concerned about choosing the right words. "Not all rules are written."

"And you're not one to follow rules."

Ceony's boldness surprised even her, and she dared not even glance at the paper magician to gauge his reaction. The air thickened and swirled around her like the vegetable broth, but instead of cooling, it seemed to grow ever hotter.

I'm his apprentice, she thought. As if he needed to remind her! And how could he possibly ask her why she did any of the things she did? She had confessed her feelings to him in the fourth chamber of his heart, after all.

She closed her eyes and pressed the back of her hand to her cheeks, willing them cool. *Fine*, she thought, letting the broth settle. *If he wants just an apprentice, I'll be just an apprentice.*

Perhaps it had been foolish of her to expect anything more.

She handed him the bowl. "I've only done three links for that shrinking chain," she said. "When you're feeling well, I'd like you to inspect them. I'd rather not spend time constructing a flawed chain. And I have some reading to do. I'll come check on you in an hour."

Ceony stood and brushed off her skirt, then *calmly* fled to her room to read her book on origami behind a closed door, where no one but her would see that awful, vibrant pink that tainted her skin.

And, for the third time that week, she did an excellent job of staying calm. By the time she finished her textbook, only two tears stained its pages.

CHAPTER 8

CEONY SAT IN A small lobby in the Parliament building on a red velvet chair. Overhead hung a golden chandelier three tiers high, haphazardly festooned with raindrop-shaped crystals. The statue of a long-dead politician watched her from the corner, standing between two copper-colored alcoves decorated with exotic ferns in large, ceramic vases. Tall circle-top windows—composed of smaller circle-top windows bunched together—let in the late-morning light, which shined white thanks to the thin, wispy clouds frosting the sky. The portrait of a past king who looked nothing like Edward VII stood some twelve feet high against the wall opposite the window, and long lines of gold leaf crisscrossed the ceiling. It may have been the fanciest waiting room Ceony had ever seen in her life, but it was still a waiting room.

The tall door behind her shut, underlining the fact that she was forbidden from attending the meeting with Criminal Affairs, to which both Emery and Mg. Aviosky had been invited. She frowned, the exile itching under her skin. She had dealt with Excisioners firsthand, *she* was the target of all this horrid hoopla, and yet she wasn't permitted to sit in on the discussion that would determine the Cabinet's plan of action! She would never understand the workings of the Cabinet, and she had still not forgiven Emery for not arguing on her behalf.

For not trusting me, she thought.

She passed a scornful glance to the new set of textbooks on the table beside her that Emery had instructed her to read: *From Pulp to Paper: The Making of a Master Craft*, *Advanced Geometry*, and *Mammals of the Cold North*, which she assumed tied into advanced animation. She harrumphed. At least she had grabbed a copy of *The Railway Magazine* from the reception area. The article "How Smelted Tie Plates Can Make Your Trips Smoother and Faster" looked somewhat interesting. She wondered if the writers would actually give away the new spells in the article.

Delilah, a fellow exile from the meeting, strolled over from the politician's statue. She had been reading the plaque with apparent interest. Her hands were clasped behind her back and her yellow skirt bounced about her calves. Today she had pinned her bobbed hair behind each ear and wore lipstick. Ceony felt rather plain in comparison with the always-flamboyant Delilah, which only upset her more.

"It's not so bad, waiting," Delilah said.

From behind the closed doors, someone—it sounded like Mg. Hughes—shouted something unintelligible.

"See?" Delilah offered with a half smile.

Ceony sighed and gestured to the chair on the other side of her. "No, I don't. Grath talked to me just *yesterday*, Delilah. I should be in there. If Magician Thane hadn't overheard everything, I probably would be."

Delilah's dark eyes bugged. So, Mg. Aviosky *hadn't* told her of the events in the twelfth-floor flat.

Mg. Aviosky had arrived at the apartment with Mg. Hughes yesterday afternoon, looking more disgruntled than Ceony had ever seen her. She'd confirmed that Grath shouldn't be able to pinpoint the flat's precise location from the mirror-to-mirror communication, though he would know they were hiding in London. Ultimately it had been Emery's decision not to move.

It took a great deal of convincing to get Mg. Hughes to believe that Grath Cobalt had indeed revealed himself as a Gaffer. Ceony suspected the Siper's ego still hadn't healed from the blow. After all, if anyone should have discovered Grath's secret, it should have been the head of Criminal Affairs.

Leaning forward and whispering, Ceony told Delilah everything, short of the stiff conversation she'd had with Emery afterward, from which she still reeled. Ceony told Delilah about the tapping, what Grath had said—verbatim—the rippling of the glass, and the blind boxes.

"And he definitely can't find me, right?"

Delilah looked pale, but she nodded. "You *can* track a person down through mirror-to-mirror communication, but not so as you'd find them on a map. He knows the mirror's signature without knowing its exact location, if that makes sense. And I think you're safe enough now that the mirror has shattered."

"Signature?" Ceony repeated.

Delilah nodded and rubbed gooseflesh from her arms. "It's like how each person has a name; each mirror has its own identity, and you can randomly mirror-hop by changing that identity. It took me three months just to learn that, so I don't know if I can explain it to you in one sitting. But knowing a mirror's location helps immensely, as does having a mirror that belonged to the person you wish to find. Grath probably knew to look in London, and with that makeup compact . . . Oh, Ceony, how frightful. This is a bad bedtime story come to life! I don't envy you at all, not one bit."

"I've had worse," Ceony said, and so far, the statement had proved true. But Ceony was gradually learning that Grath was far different than Lira, and while facing a Gaffer and an Excisioner seemed less terrifying than facing *two* Excisioners, Ceony was beginning to wonder if she'd finally dug in too deep.

"He's the Gaffer," Ceony said. "There was no one in the room with him. But a man doesn't have to have dark magic to do dark things."

"At least you broke the mirror before he transported," Delilah offered.

"How does it work?" Ceony asked, scooting forward in her chair. "How can a person step from one mirror into another?"

Delilah frowned, but she sifted through her large purse and pulled out her own compact makeup mirror, then another small, rectangular mirror, about the length of Ceony's hand. Ceony heard the clinking of glass beads in the bag, and she wondered how much glass the Gaffer apprentice carried with her. Paper had its downfalls, but at least it transported easily.

She handed the rectangular mirror to Ceony. "I'm already familiar with that mirror, so this will be easy," she said, opening her makeup compact. She said, "Search, quad three."

"That's the signature?" Ceony whispered as she looked at the mirror. Her reflection swirled until the glass showed Delilah's face instead. Ceony glanced over and spied herself in Delilah's mirror. The mirrors reflected each other.

"I renamed it for the sake of ease," Delilah said. "Otherwise it's more of a thought."

Ceony nodded, not quite understanding. Glass magic seemed far different from Folding.

Another raised voice, this one unfamiliar, echoed behind the closed doors, but Ceony ignored it.

"So that's that," Delilah said, her voice sounding from both her physical body and the small mirror in Ceony's hand. "Transport is trickier," she explained, and she traced the tip of her right index finger around the compact mirror clockwise, then counterclockwise, and finally clockwise again. She said, "Transport, pass through."

The two mirrors rippled as the vanity room mirror had done yesterday. Delilah pushed her index finger through the glass of her mirror. It bulged out of Ceony's mirror, protruding like a severed limb. Delilah wiggled it, and Ceony laughed.

"It doesn't work with imperfect mirrors," Delilah said, withdrawing her finger. She said, "Cease," and the mirrors returned to their normal states. "You can get trapped trying to use an imperfect mirror. Scratches, breaks, even tiny bubbles can act as boulders and nooses when you try to pass through. Aviosky only lets me transport using Gaffer mirrors, because it's not safe otherwise."

"She sounds like a strict teacher," Ceony said, handing the rectangular mirror back.

Delilah stowed both mirrors in her purse. "She is, but it's been good for me. I need some structure in my life." She smiled. "I think I'm going to try and test for my magicianship at the end of the year. I think I'll pass if I study hard between now and then."

"I think so, too," Ceony said.

Delilah nodded, then grew oddly quiet. Quiet enough that Ceony could hear stifled mumbling from behind the closed doors. She wondered just what aspect of her problems the magicians were discussing.

After a long moment, Delilah said, "They're going to focus their search on Saraj, not Grath. I overheard Magician Aviosky on her mirror this morning. I think she was talking to Magician Hughes or one of his associates. Magician Cantrell, maybe."

Ceony drew her brows together. "But Grath is the ringleader! He's the one who—"

"They're awful stories, Ceony," Delilah interrupted, her voice half a whisper. She glanced to the closed doors before leaning in and saying, "I looked them up at the library, after your buggy accident. Magician Aviosky wouldn't tell me anything, so I did some research of my own. The news articles alone . . ."

Delilah shivered. "They don't say everything, but they say enough. Whole families murdered, strange runes drawn in blood, and . . ." She paled. "Saraj has killed babies, Ceony. He attacked an orphanage and killed twenty-three kids, but he only"—she swallowed—"*harvested* five of them. He just killed the others for sport. He's like a rabid animal. Grath takes credit for a lot—and yes, I think he's sort of in charge—but he's not even an Excisioner. I think . . . I think that's why they're going after Saraj. Whoever Magician Aviosky talked to this morning thinks he's the one who's responsible for the mill and what happened to your buggy. He's too much of a public threat to leave alone. He said Grath is 'containable.'"

Ceony's pulse pounded in her ears, and for a moment she heard nothing else. So much death, so much horror. She thought of the buggy driver, an innocent stranger. How easily the man in the night—this Saraj Prendi—had killed him. Saraj probably followed all the buggy drivers, touching each one, to make sure his spell would work the night of the accident.

She sat back in her chair, cold. How long had he watched the cottage to ensure he was there when Ceony and Emery left? How many more people could be hurt—killed—because of her involvement with Lira?

The list of casualties from the paper mill surfaced in her mind, and she reminded herself of each and every name. Had she not gotten involved with Lira—had she not *frozen* her—Grath and Saraj wouldn't have come to London, to Dartford. All those people would still be alive. Though Ceony hadn't set off the bomb or killed the driver of her buggy, all the violent deaths weighed on her shoulders. *She* was the reason these two murderers had infiltrated England.

Her glance passed to the closed doors. Emery could have been killed in that accident. He could have been hurt at the mill, had he come, or at the flat, had Grath's timing been different. It was a miracle either of them still breathed.

It was her fault. And she hated it.

The two apprentices sat in silence for a long moment, Delilah staring out the window, Ceony drumming her fingers on the velvet armrests of her chair. She mulled over her conversations with Grath and everything that had happened with Lira, from when the Excisioner nearly broke her back in Emery's kitchen to the end, when Ceony read those fateful words from the bloodied paper in her hands: "Lira froze."

Now Lira had as little life in her as the statue of the politician that stood staring at Ceony from across the room. Ceony had done that. By chance, but she had done it. Because Emery had been in trouble. Because Emery hadn't deserved to die. Because, maybe, some tiny part of her had loved him from the first moment they met. But she had done it, and she had done it alone.

A chill coursed up Ceony's arms. "It's my responsibility to fix this," she whispered.

Delilah turned from the window. "What?"

"My fault, my responsibility," Ceony mumbled, withdrawing her arms from the armrests and folding her hands in her lap. "I defeated Lira; I should be the one to handle Saraj and Grath, too."

She'd faced an Excisioner before and won, hadn't she? Couldn't she do it again?

Delilah yelped, a sort of strange hiccup. She clapped one hand over her mouth, wide-eyed, then dropped it back into her lap. "No, Ceony. You can't be serious."

"I'm not much of a comedian, I'm afraid," she replied. Her fingers trembled, but she curled them into fists and took a deep breath. "I don't know about Saraj, but I think I could contact Grath. Lure him out. He's only a Gaffer, after all. I'll need your help, Delilah. Can you trace the mirror he used to contact me?"

Delilah's expression turned wan and colorless. "I . . . I wouldn't even know where to start! And I'm only an apprentice—"

"The mirror from my vanity room," Ceony said in a hushed voice. "The pieces are all still there. Could you trace him through that?"

Delilah opened her mouth to respond, then closed it. She glanced at the closed doors that concealed the Criminal Affairs department.

Voice like a frog's, she said, "I think so, but we'd have to get a ride there—"

"Not if we transport," Ceony said, courage beginning to form in her chest. She couldn't afford to sit and wait for something else to happen. She had to fight. She had to stop Grath before any more tombstones went up on her behalf. "Surely Parliament wouldn't install flawed mirrors. There's one in the ladies' room. We could use that to transport to the lobby of my apartment."

"But Magician Aviosky—"

"If anything goes amiss, we can form a new plan," Ceony said. She scooted forward and grasped Delilah's hands. "You can stand out of the way, so Grath will never see you, only me. I just need to talk to him. He wanted to negotiate with Lira, remember? Well, I'll make him think I'm ready to negotiate. And if we contact him through one of the shards of the mirror I broke at the apartment, he won't be able to transport through it.

"Don't you see, Delilah?" she asked. "I need to wrap up this mess before anyone else gets hurt. I can do it. I know I can. But we have to leave now, while there's still time."

"What do you plan to say to him?"

"I guess that depends on what he says to me," she confessed. "I want to know his plans. I'll say all the right things, and hopefully he'll reveal a weak spot, a way for us to thwart him."

Delilah bit her lip, but nodded. "You sound like a real magician. Okay. But we have to hurry."

Ceony jumped up from her chair and linked arms with Delilah, pulling her toward the ladies' room.

This is my fight now, she thought, hurrying from the lobby, *my chance of atonement. It's time to end this, once and for all.*

CHAPTER 9

THE WOMEN'S LAVATORY, WHICH was composed of two rooms, looked just as elegant as the lobby. The entry opened onto a small sitting area illuminated by a frosted window dressed in maroon drapes, as well as a small white-crystal chandelier buzzing with electric lights. Wallpaper adorned with yellow cowslips covered the walls, trimmed at ceiling and floor by a narrow maroon border. A glass makeup stand rested in the corner with a rosewood bench and small, round mirror, and a narrow dresser sat against the west wall between two cushioned chairs. Above the dresser hung a large, rectangular mirror in a gold frame. Exotic ferns decorated the other corners of the room. The next room held a few modest stalls.

Ceony approached the larger mirror, checking its surface for any flaws, though she felt sure she was looking for all the wrong things. Delilah chewed on her thumbnail, looking even more distraught than she had in the lobby.

Ceony turned to her. "Will it work?"

Delilah approached the mirror and gave it a quick perusal. "Well, it *should*, but . . ."

She didn't finish the sentence, only reached out and tapped her nails against the glass, first in the center, then on the edges.

"Please, Delilah," Ceony begged. "Can you find the mirror in the lobby of my complex?"

Delilah nodded. "I might as well act like a real magician, too," she said. She pressed her hands to the glass and closed her eyes. "Search," she said, and the mirror fogged beneath her touch. The image began to flash from image to image. Ceony could only suppose they were reflections of other mirrors in the city; she saw a white dust cloth, a cluttered attic, two little girls sitting in a pink-painted room having a tea party. She saw the startled face of a man, a woman desperately trying to zip up the back of her dress, and then the staircase in the lobby of her block of flats.

"There, there!" Ceony cried, and Delilah ripped her hands from the mirror, taking a step back to see for herself.

Ceony recognized the walnut-glazed staircase, the short table holding both a telephone and a telegraph, the slip of hallway on the edge of the picture that led back into the landlord's rooms. The mirror hung on the wall near the receiving desk. If Ceony could stick her head through it and look to the left, she'd see the front doors of the building.

"Can they see us?" Ceony asked.

"Anyone who walks by will," Delilah said. She heaved a deep breath and said, "Well, come on. Let's hurry before we're caught."

Delilah pulled over one of the cushioned chairs and stood on it, then traced the tip of her right index finger just inside the mirror's gilded frame clockwise, counterclockwise, then clockwise again. She said, "Transport, pass through."

The image of the lobby shivered and faded, and the glass of the lavatory mirror started to ripple.

"I hope the mirror on the other side is big enough," Delilah said.

"It is," Ceony promised.

Delilah grabbed her hand, sucked in another breath, and held it. She stepped up on the dresser—pulling Ceony onto the chair, their hands still linked together—and slowly slipped through the silvery glass.

Ceony squeezed her friend's hand tighter and gasped at the coldness of the glass as her hand, arm, and shoulder squeezed through it. She closed her eyes as the rest of her body slipped onto the other side. It felt wet, yet the wetness didn't stick. The lighting around her changed to a more orange tone, and she tripped as she tumbled down from the frame of the lobby's mirror. Delilah steadied her.

Ceony opened her eyes and parted her lips in wonder. She really *was* standing in the lobby of her block of flats!

Whirling back to face the mirror, Ceony saw it ripple for only half a second before the glass returned to normal, reflecting her image and Delilah's, not the Parliament lavatory.

Ceony cried out and flung her arms around Delilah.

"Amazing!" she said, stepping back just as quickly. "I can't believe you can do that! How remarkable to be a Gaffer, Delilah!"

Delilah smiled. "Not a Gaffer yet, technically."

Ceony grabbed Delilah's hand and pulled her past the stairs to the lift, ignoring the wide-eyed stare of a man who had obviously witnessed them pop out of the mirror as easily as if it had been a door. She drew the lift doors shut, but as it slowly climbed to the twelfth floor, her excitement about mirror-to-mirror transport gradually slipped away, replaced by a stirring anxiety.

Grath.

Her fingers trembled slightly as she fished out her key and opened the door to her and Emery's temporary abode. Nothing had changed from that morning. Fennel looked up expectantly from the couch, where it appeared he had been sleeping.

"You keep quiet about this, boy," Ceony said just above a whisper. She tugged Delilah inside, locked the door behind her, and led the way to the vanity room.

The room had remained untouched since Ceony had tucked the pieces of shattered glass into the three blind boxes. She left the door open and knelt by the first blind box, handling it with care.

"So, none of these are big enough for someone to pass through, right?" she said.

Delilah nodded. "Yes, he can't come through anymore. At least not using this mirror."

Ceony nodded. Opening the lid of the blind box, she carefully lifted one piece of the mirror out, an oblong triangle with sharp edges and one chipped corner. It measured just larger than her hand. She shut the blind box and handed the piece to Delilah.

Delilah turned it over in her hands, then set it on the floor. "I'll do the spells, Ceony, but I don't want him to see me."

"He did, once. At the bistro."

Delilah shuddered. "Well, I don't want him to see me again."

Ceony nodded. Delilah pressed her fingers to the glass, then scooted away so that the shard of mirror didn't reflect her face. Ceony hovered over it instead, staring into her own reflection, shadowed and blue from the filtered light passing through the room's window.

"Reflect, past," Delilah ordered, and Ceony's reflection changed to a wide view of the vanity room.

Ceony licked her lips. "It can show you what happened in this room before?"

Delilah nodded and whispered, "It's handy for detective work. Magician Aviosky used to serve on the police force before transferring to Tagis Praff."

"Really?"

Delilah nodded, then returned her focus to the work at hand. "Search, Ceony Small," she said. To Ceony, she whispered, "Your compact. I named it so we could chat long distance."

She smiled. "That's sweet."

"Reverse," Delilah commanded the mirror, in a voice as bold as a mouse's.

The image in the glass changed, and in it Ceony could see the foot of a bed and a wardrobe—the same room where Grath had stood before. Her makeup mirror must have been sitting in the middle of the mattress. She heard voices coming from the part of the room she couldn't see and leaned in closer to the mirror so she could hear them better.

"Hold," Delilah whispered.

"—can't keep going behind my back!" Grath hissed. Ceony recognized his voice immediately.

She didn't recognize the voice that responded, smooth as chocolate and with a strange accent that clipped most of his vowels and swallowed half his consonants: "How long have we been in England?" he asked, his voice quieter than Grath's, more *practiced*. Ceony had to press her ear to the glass to hear, and her drumming heart only made it that much harder to listen. "We were supposed to sail for Gibraltar three months ago. Your plan, if you remember."

"I've talked to wild dogs that make me repeat myself less than you do, Saraj."

Ceony stiffened and glanced to Delilah, whose eyes widened until they shined more white than brown.

In her stupor, Ceony missed the first few words of Saraj's response. "—lost interest now. You promised me a good game, but there's no excitement here." He paused. "Let's get the bird gone and sail. I hear African blood makes for a strong aphrodisiac."

She could sense the Excisioner's smile. Her every limb shivered.

"I don't want her dead!" Grath shouted. Ceony jerked back from the mirror shard, and Delilah nearly released it. "Not yet. We still—"

"Find yourself some new meat," Saraj replied, tone darkening. "You're on your own. I'm—"

"Shhh," Grath hissed.

Saraj said nothing, and a moment later the view in the mirror changed, shifting to show the front of the wardrobe and the hinges on the room's door. Grath had picked it up.

Ceony shouted into the mirror, hoping it would make Grath think she'd only just tapped into it. "Grath! Are you there?" she called. "I've got your magic. Let's talk!"

To her relief, he chuckled. Gooseflesh instantly tickled her arms and legs. The image in the mirror shifted and darkened, revealing Grath's face. His burn had completely healed. Had Saraj done that?

Delilah cowered, but kept her hands on the mirror. Grath blocked off the rest of the room behind him, including all signs of Saraj.

"And the little bird returns," Grath said. His eyes shifted left and right, as though he were trying to peer past Ceony. "What Gaffer have you gotten to help you, hmm? Brave man."

"It's none of your concern," Ceony snapped, talking louder than necessary to keep her voice from shaking. "I'm ready to negotiate."

Grath laughed again. Ceony kept her face smooth, though she couldn't help but purse her lips. She knew negotiating with a killer was worthless—she wasn't completely dim-witted. Still, it could only be to her benefit if he thought her naïve. Naïveté seemed the strongest card Ceony had to play, and she knew how to cheat at cards.

"I admit I wasn't expecting cooperation," Grath said, pitching his voice low.

"I'm only cooperating if you leave Saraj Prendi out of the picture," Ceony said. "This is between you and me."

Grath frowned. A vein in his forehead popped and pulsed, and

Ceony thought she heard the closing of a door behind him. Had the Excisioner left?

"That man is a real tosser," Grath said, grinning wide enough to reveal his sharp canines, but that vein still throbbed in his forehead. His ears had turned red as well. "I'll take care of him, pet. Don't you worry. *I* don't want you dead, not yet. Not when you still have information I need."

Delilah whimpered. Ceony gestured for her to stay quiet.

"Good. I'm glad we're already in agreement," she said.

The vein on Grath's forehead smoothed. "I'm listening. Talk."

"Not that easy," Ceony said. "I want a guarantee that Saraj leaves us alone. In fact, the farther away he goes, the better." *Gibraltar, Africa, I don't care. Just get him away.*

"Us?" Grath repeated. "You and Thane?"

"Us, as in everyone who lives here," Ceony snapped. "Think outside the frame, Grath."

He chuckled. "I get Saraj out, and you tell me your little secrets."

"And I want you out, too," Ceony said. "I'll give you what you want, but I want you—and Lira—gone for good." *Preferably in a jail cell, if I can swing this right.*

Grath hesitated for a moment, but said, "Done."

Ceony tried to hide her surprise. Grath sounded sincere; would he and Saraj really leave if Ceony restored Lira? No, she didn't even need to restore her, only tell Grath how she froze her in the first place. She didn't think that information could be used for ill, at least not by a Gaffer.

What are you thinking? she chided herself. *You can't actually give that information away. Just make him beg for it long enough to expose his weakness.*

At least it sounded like Saraj wanted to leave anyway. A small relief, albeit an uneasy one. Who would the Excisioner hurt next?

She turned the bargain over in her mind, kneading it like bread dough. Could she get Grath's defenses down long enough to do him in?

"Having second thoughts?" Grath asked. "Too late to back out, dearie. We do this now, or I'll have Saraj hurt you bad, you hear? You've got a family in town? Parents? A cute sister, maybe?"

Ceony's heart hammered. Her chest felt cold. She swallowed and took a deep breath, trying to hide her frayed nerves, her panic. "Wh-Where is Lira?"

"I can take you there," the Gaffer said. He backed off from the mirror by a few inches. "Tell me where you are."

"I'll meet you there," Ceony countered. She pulled up Emery's schedule from her memory—he had a meeting with Parliament again tomorrow, at one o'clock. Another meeting Ceony couldn't attend. The timing was perfect.

"Tomorrow, after lunch," she said. "I don't like cooperating on an empty stomach. One thirty."

Delilah's eyes bugged. She tried to gesture something to Ceony without taking her hands off the mirror, but Ceony ignored her.

Grath chuckled. "There's an abandoned barn outside of the city, south. If you take Hangman's Road to the fork, and the dirt street west, you'll see it. Off the road, at the base of the hills. Come by yourself, because if I so much as see a driver with you, I'll find that blond piece from the restaurant and have some fun with her. Understand?"

Delilah paled, but thankfully didn't break the spell.

Ceony cleared her throat before answering. "Clear as Gaffer's glass. Same to you."

Grath laughed again. "And what will a Folder do to me, hmm?"

"I'm more than a Folder, remember?" Ceony lied. She made a sharp gesture to Delilah, who whispered, "Cease." Grath's image vanished, and the mirror reflected only Ceony's face.

Ceony scooped the shard of mirror off the floor and shoved it into the blind box, breathing like she had just run up ten flights of stairs.

"You can't!" Delilah cried, tears on her eyelashes. "You can't possibly meet with him! You have to tell the magicians!"

"And let you get hurt? Or my family?" Ceony shot back. "Do you think he was kidding about Saraj? I told you, Delilah, this is *my* fight now." She wrung her hands together, trying to ignore the feeling of dripping oil inside her stomach. "I just have to be prepared."

Delilah nodded. "Prepared, okay. We . . . we can do this."

Ceony sat back, propping herself up with her hands, and thought for a long moment. "We need to outsmart him, and form a plan for if things don't go well," she said. "But if I can get rid of them, I'll do it. I have to."

"Can you set a trap?" Delilah asked. "Something . . . papery?"

Ceony perked up. "Can you take me to the cottage, Delilah? To Magician Thane's house?"

Wrinkles creased her forehead. "What do you need there?"

"A giant glider," Ceony said. "And a paper doll."

CHAPTER 10

AFTER SPENDING THE NEXT hour mirror-hopping, Ceony and Delilah rushed back into the Parliament lobby, receiving several quizzical looks from the red-clad foot guards monitoring the hall-ways. Immense relief washed over Ceony at the sight of the closed doors. Mg. Hughes was speaking loudly on the other side. She sank into her red velvet chair to keep from getting dizzy.

Delilah scuttled to the other chair like a crab, moving sideways as she stared at the doors. They didn't open, and Delilah sat without consequence.

Ceony leaned forward, seized Delilah's wrist, and said, "Promise me you won't say a word."

"But—"

"Not a word!" she hissed, glancing back to the doors herself. Had she heard a chair scooting back, or was she imagining things? It didn't matter. They would have no way of knowing what she and Delilah had been doing.

She took a deep breath. Knowing Emery, he'd pick up on something if she didn't act completely calm. She could play up her frustration at being excluded from the meeting if need be.

Pinning her gaze on Delilah again, Ceony said, "Promise me."

Delilah wilted. "I promise," she mumbled. "Oh, Ceony, had I known you better at Praff, I never would have passed my final exam!" She hiccupped. "Now I have heartburn."

The right door to the meeting room opened from within, and a man Ceony only knew as a Polymaker—a plastics magician—stepped out, his attention still on the room within. Empty chairs now surrounded the oval table, but magicians and several uniformed policemen clustered about it in twos and threes, mumbling to one another.

Scooting closer to Delilah, Ceony whispered, "Don't forget tomorrow."

Delilah rubbed her palms up and down her arms. "But where will we do it?"

"The lavatory," Ceony said, glancing at the conference room. The clusters of people were beginning to break up and inch toward the door. "There's a lock on the door in the lavatory, from the inside."

Magicians began to filter into the lobby. Ceony snapped back from Delilah and smoothed her hair, noting that her braid looked a little tousled. A person didn't get a tousled braid from sitting idly in a chair all morning long.

Would Emery notice? Ceony couldn't help but wonder how much Emery noticed about her at all. Their conversation in the flat's living room still sat uneasily with her.

She kept her eyes on the conference room doors, watching as Mg. Hughes stepped out into the foyer and started talking with another man she didn't know. Mg. Cantrell—the Smelter who had interrogated Emery after the buggy crashed into the river—followed behind.

Delilah popped up from her chair like a spring, clutching her bag as if she had stolen it as Mg. Aviosky and Emery made their way over. Ceony resisted reaction—she prayed Delilah wouldn't give them away with her body language alone.

"I apologize for the delay," Mg. Aviosky said, glancing behind her shoulder to Mg. Hughes. "Some of us are especially long-winded."

Ceony faked a yawn and covered it with a hand. "It *was* long, and those books are tiresome. I assume I'll hear nothing of what you decided without me?"

Emery frowned—it only showed in his eyes—but before he could respond, Mg. Aviosky answered, "Correct, Miss Twill. The less you know, the safer you are. I'll be sure to have you debriefed once things have been settled."

Emery picked up Ceony's stack of books and cradled them in the crook of one arm, then rested his other hand on her shoulder. "Let's go back. We have some things to review."

Mg. Aviosky cleared her throat, and Ceony noticed that her spectacles-framed gaze rested solidly on Emery's hand. It quickly moved up to Emery's face.

"If you don't mind, Magician Thane, I'd like to speak to Ceony privately for a moment," she said. "Only a moment."

Ceony's stomach dropped about half an inch. She feared she knew what Mg. Aviosky wanted to discuss and took great effort not to make eye contact with Emery.

Delilah looked worried.

"Very well," Emery said, removing his hand. To Ceony he said, "I'll be outside."

"Delilah, if you'll wait here," Mg. Aviosky said as Emery left. "Miss Twill, this way."

Ceony, stomach dropping a little more, followed two paces behind Mg. Aviosky. Ironically enough, they ended up in the women's lavatory where Delilah had worked her magic just moments before.

Ceony made a point of not looking at the mirror. Mg. Aviosky gestured to the chair they'd used to scramble up the dresser. Ceony sat without word.

"When I assigned you to be a Folder," Mg. Aviosky began, her hands clasped behind her back as she paced back and forth, "I debriefed you on the proper apprenticely conduct and what was expected of you once you began your employment under Magician Thane."

Trying to keep her brow smooth, Ceony nodded.

"Perhaps there are a few things I forgot to mention," Mg. Aviosky said, taking a moment to push her round-framed spectacles up higher on her nose. "Such as referring to a magician by his first name."

Ceony flushed. "I . . . I didn't mean to do it, it's just—"

"I'll tell you now that I do not like mixed sexes in magician-apprentice relationships," Mg. Aviosky went on, "and I do not assign them unless I deem it necessary, which in your case, it was. Eleven of our twelve Folders are male, and the only female already has an apprentice."

Ceony touched a hand to her cheek in a feeble attempt to cool it. In all her daydreams regarding Emery, nothing quite this humiliating had ever happened.

"I believe you and Magician Thane are entirely too familiar with each other," Mg. Aviosky continued, glancing at Ceony briefly before switching her focus to one of the lavatory's ferns. "Which I do not credit entirely to you, Miss Twill. I'm not here to scold you, only to warn and protect you."

Ceony slid forward on her chair. "Protect me? What exactly do you suspect Magician Thane would do?" She paled. "Mercy in heaven, have you spoken to him about this?"

"No, I have not," the Gaffer clarified. "I wanted to speak with you first."

Ceony released a long breath of air, offering silent thanks that she had been saved that embarrassment, at least.

She slumped in her chair, gaze dropping to the floor.

"Why do you do all of this for me, Ceony?"

"You know why."

She swallowed hard, feeling like a stroke of paint on a canvas far too large for her to comprehend.

Mg. Aviosky said, "I think it's in your best interest—and Magician Thane's—if I transfer you."

Ceony's stomach sunk to her ankles.

"I've seen to the arrangements," Mg. Aviosky continued. "Magician Howard's apprentice isn't expected to advance until the end of the summer, but she's agreed to take on a second apprentice in order to boost our Folder numbers. I think you'll find her to be very amicable, and—"

"I don't want to transfer," Ceony interrupted, her brow thoroughly knit now. "I told you before that I want to continue learning from Magician Thane."

Mg. Aviosky frowned. "And as *I've* said, you two are far too familiar with each other. I see things you don't think I see—"

"Like what?" Ceony blurted, standing.

"And as the administrator of apprenticeships," she continued, "I am making the decision to transfer you, once I finalize the arrangements and speak to—"

"Of course I'm *familiar* with him!" Ceony said, raising her voice and cutting off Mg. Aviosky's words clean at the preposition. "I live with him! I learn from him! I've *walked through his heart*, Aviosky! You *know* that!"

"Yes," Mg. Aviosky said, stiff. "I recall. I also recall you were both incredibly vague about just what you experienced there, which only fuels my concern."

Ceony shook her head. She felt hot, as if her own pulse were steadily bringing her blood to a boil. "It doesn't matter. What matters is—"

"I will decide what does and doesn't matter, Miss Twill!" Mg. Aviosky shot back.

"No!" she shouted, loud enough that Mg. Aviosky retreated a step. "You don't understand what it was like in there. You *can't* understand what happened! I know his heart better than my own, don't you see?"

Mg. Aviosky didn't respond.

"I feel like I've known him all my life," Ceony continued, quieter now. "Like he was always meant to be a part of it. And Folding . . . I love Folding because *he* taught it to me, because *he* showed me the beauty in simple things. The beauty I have within myself."

"Miss Twill—"

"I love him," Ceony said, and Mg. Aviosky's eyes widened almost to the size of polo balls. "And it's as though I've always loved him. As though that feeble paper heart I gave him were my own . . ."

She paused, realizing she had said too much. She had stunned Mg. Aviosky into silence.

Ceony stood straighter and forced herself to speak calmly. "I haven't broken any rules," she said. "I'm well versed on them. I could recite them to you verbatim, if necessary. Until I break a rule, it's unnecessary for you to take any action, especially as drastic as this. I believe that's something on which we both can agree."

Mg. Aviosky pursed her lips.

"For now," Ceony said, her tone as formal as she could make it, "I would like to continue studying under Magician Thane."

Ceony walked to the door, but before opening it, she said, "If it makes a difference, I'm sure Magician Thane would not give you a similar speech. I can assure you my infatuation is entirely one-sided."

Ceony hurried back into the hallway, which felt significantly cooler than the lavatory. She pressed both hands to her cheeks, then her neck, urging her skin to cool. She pinched the front of her blouse and shook it to get some air. Her heels clicked loudly against the hallway's tiled floor.

She blinked rapidly to avoid crying. How dare Mg. Aviosky stick her nose where it didn't belong!

She sucked in a deep breath and held it for several steps.

Her shoulders remembered the weight of Emery's arm around them, and she could feel the warm press of his lips against her forehead as she shivered in the black waters of the river by the cottage. She thought of how he often wore an inscrutable expression to conceal his thoughts, of the late nights he spent in contemplation. What did he conceal behind those mindful expressions, those unreadable glances?

Entirely one-sided. But was it?

She banished the thoughts from her mind and swallowed the small lump forming in her throat. Now was not the time for girlish ponderings.

Glancing over her shoulder, Ceony saw no sign of Mg. Aviosky, but she did catch Delilah's eye. Ceony must have looked a wreck judging from the way Delilah's face scrunched. Ceony managed a nod—they were safe, as far as Grath went—and turned away, fanning herself with both hands. Giving herself a moment to calm down.

Emery was waiting just outside Parliament's east doors, standing by a buggy, apparently having a conversation with the driver. When he saw Ceony, his eyes narrowed.

The driver hurried around to his side of the car. Emery met Ceony halfway and asked, "What's wrong?"

Ceony shook her head and stepped past him. "It's nothing," she said. "Just Magician Aviosky being herself."

The concern didn't leave his green eyes—if anything, it intensified—but he didn't push for an answer. Reaching around Ceony, he opened the door to the buggy and helped her in.

It was a long, silent ride home.

CHAPTER 11

CEONY, LEANING AGAINST THE cover of her origami textbook, carefully aligned the edges of her full-point Fold before setting the crease with her thumbnail. She lifted the newly formed triangle and opened it up, then pressed it down into a square Fold. It was the fourth crane-style bird she had Folded, for she knew from experience one could never have too many paper birds.

A knock sounded at her bedroom door; Ceony glanced under the bed—ensuring her secrets were well concealed—before saying, "Come in."

Emery opened the door and took two steps into her room—a threshold he had only begun crossing one month ago. He eyed the partially formed bird in Ceony's hands, the birds beside her, the links of a shield chain, and likely the Folded stars, bats, and Ripple spell scattered over the floor. Ceony hadn't bothered to hide those; she figured it would look less suspicious with everything out in the open.

"You've been busy," he commented, scratching the back of his head. "And here I thought I wasn't giving you enough free time."

Ceony flipped her paper over and formed another square Fold. "I do plan to test for my magicianship at two years," she said. "I need to practice if I'm to pass."

Emery smiled without teeth, but his eyes showed something else—nostalgia, or something similar. Dolefulness, maybe?

"So ready to leave?" he asked.

Ceony paused in her Folding. "It's not like that—"

"I know," he said, and the look disappeared, his eyes masking whatever shadows played about that light in his head.

Ceony hated it when he did that.

He rescanned the room, perhaps frowning inwardly at the lack of organization in Ceony's work. "Do keep in touch, after the magicianship," he said. "I'd be surprised if it took you more than two years."

Ceony kept her focus on her bird. *Are you saying that because it's what you want, or because it's the polite thing to say?* she wondered.

Emery stepped back into the living room, closing Ceony's door with a delicate touch. Ceony formed two chicken Folds before retrieving her scissors and her paper doll—stolen back from the cottage—from under her bed. She needed to make every possible preparation before facing Grath tomorrow.

She had nearly finished. Two more snips, and the silhouette would be free. If Ceony cut it out correctly, the spell would work. If not, she'd have to start over from scratch, but she didn't have time to do that before her one thirty appointment tomorrow.

Chewing on her lower lip, Ceony carefully cut the line at the doll's right hip. It fell away from its bordering paper.

Ceony grasped the doll by the shoulders and stood, taking it to the bedroom closet, away from direct line of sight of the door, as the bedroom didn't have a lock. She straightened it as best she could, the two-dimensional head flopping, and said, "Stand."

To her relief and exuberance, the paper cutout stiffened and stood on its own accord, feeling almost like thin cardboard. She released its shoulders.

Now for the real test. Mimicking Emery's demonstration of the spell, she stood two feet away from the doll, arranged herself to match the silhouette, and said, "Copy."

Wispy color—similar to that of a story illusion—began to form on the doll. Orange glazed the head; the shirt turned gray, the skirt, navy. The colors molded and darkened until a perfect, flat replica of Ceony stood across from her. It bore the same hopeful expression Ceony must have been wearing when she gave the "Copy" command. Even the backside of the doll matched Ceony's backside. From straight on, it looked like a real person. From any other view, it was obviously a paper doll.

Ceony stepped back and sat on her bed, studying her work. A decent illusion, for paper, though the doll couldn't speak, and its interactions with its environment would be incredibly limited. It had no joints, after all, and no brain. A Gaffer could create a much better illusion, if a less opaque one. Or a Polymaker. Polymakers always made such complex things out of plastic.

She stared at the doll, her exuberance fading.

She thought of Lira.

Emery Thane's heart bore dozens of corners and alleyways that she hadn't seen during her short stay there. For instance, she knew about none of Emery's previous love interests besides Lira, whom he had married. Staring at the paper doll, Ceony couldn't help but notice the physical differences between herself and Lira.

Thanks to her keen memory, Ceony could picture Lira down to the stitches in her clothing. She pushed away thoughts of the black-clad Excisioner who had stolen Emery's heart in more ways than one, and instead pulled up the image of the woman with whom

Emery had fallen in love—the Lira from the flowery hill at sunset and from the quaint wedding where, for the briefest instant, Ceony had stood in her place.

Though Ceony hated to admit it, Lira was one of the most stunning women she had ever laid eyes on, far more stunning than what Ceony saw in the mirror. Or, in this case, in her paper doll. Lira had dark, curling hair; long, dark lashes; and dark eyes. Ceony had oddly orange hair kinked with a few awkward waves, blond eyelashes and eyebrows, and pale eyes. Lira was built like one of those girls Ceony saw on glamour photographs outside risqué theatres; Ceony had a much narrower frame, all sharper angles and straight lines. She was short, too, the top of her head measuring about equal with Emery's Adam's apple. With the right shoes, Lira could have looked him in the eye.

Ceony didn't know much about what Lira had been like before becoming an Excisioner—only that she had been a nurse and far more pleasant—but she knew she and Emery's ex-wife were very, very different people.

So how could she possibly believe that a man like Emery would fall for a simple girl like her?

Ceony fell back onto the bed and stared up at the beige ceiling. She thought again of the fortuity box she'd Folded the day Emery awoke from his Excision-induced slumber. Its vision had been as crisp as anything she'd seen in Emery's heart, yet the future was always changing. Any psychic at the county fair knew as much. Would Emery's future include her at all if she were to read it now? She didn't think she wanted to know, assuming the paper magician cared enough to humor her a second time.

Ceony pushed Lira out of her mind and thought instead of all the small moments that had fueled her hope—the signs that Emery might harbor some affection for her, too.

And Mg. Aviosky had obviously sensed something between them if she had gone so far as to set up another apprenticeship for Ceony. It couldn't all be in Ceony's head.

"You're my apprentice. I don't . . . don't think I need to remind you of that."

Ceony deflated. Or perhaps what Mg. Aviosky saw truly *was* entirely one-sided. No wonder she hadn't spoken to Emery first. Mg. Thane, that is.

Shutting her eyes, Ceony let her mind drift until it settled on a memory six weeks after her trip into the paper magician's heart. An especially hot Wednesday afternoon. It was the first moment she had thought, *Maybe this will work. Maybe I'm someone worth falling for.*

She had taken it upon herself to start a small vegetable garden in the narrow backyard of the cottage, where the soil wasn't covered in paper plants. She crouched over the small lot she had prepared, dark topsoil spread out before her and staining her gloves, the sun casting patterns over her skirt as it shined through the wicker brim of her hat. She picked herself off the ground after planting the last seeds—radishes—and bent backward so that her sore back cracked in four places.

Emery appeared beside her. "Congratulations, Ceony, you've successfully made a very large stretch of dirt."

"You'll thank me in a month or so," she countered, pulling off her gloves. "And next year you'll be begging me to make it even bigger."

Emery smiled, then reached forward and ran his thumb over Ceony's cheek, brushing off some of the dirt there. Ceony, of course, had humiliated herself by flushing redder than the tomatoes that would soon be growing at her feet.

But he hadn't moved his hand, not right away. He hesitated,

looking at her, those beautiful emerald eyes burning holes through her skin.

"Wh-What?" Ceony stuttered.

He smiled and dropped his hand. "Oh, nothing. I was just thinking about how much I like your name."

Ceony opened her eyes, bringing herself back to the present. She sat up, her gaze meeting the empty eyes of her paper doll. "Cease," she said, and the paper collapsed to the floor, losing its color in the process.

Then Ceony slid off the mattress and knelt on the floor, reaching under her bed. She hadn't been able to take much from the cottage—she would have to explain all of it, if Emery ever discovered her cache—but her fingers wrapped around a corded paper stem, and she pulled out one of the red roses Emery had crafted for her birthday, its red paper petals still perfectly crisp.

She fingered the flower's lifelike bud.

I can wait two years, she thought, turning the rose in her hand. *I can wait two years for him, longer if need be. If he would ever love me, I'd wait my entire life.*

But even two years felt like an eternity. What if Emery found someone else? Ceony could only pray they returned to the cottage soon so that the paper magician could go back to being a recluse and not meet anyone new.

She sighed and returned the rose to its hiding place. How much time she had wasted moping around like a lovesick schoolgirl!

She gathered her paper doll and stashed it away, then returned to her work. Setting the half-formed paper bird aside, she began Folding a series of small Burst spells. She could not spend more time mooning over Emery. He could wait. He *had* to wait.

For now, Ceony had to prepare. It was up to her to control the Excisioners. It was up to her to protect him, and herself.

She stayed up late Folding her spells and carefully arranging them in her bag—the same bag she had armed herself with when she faced Lira on Foulness Island.

Before she went to bed, she loaded her Tatham percussion-lock pistol and added its weight to her bounty of spells.

One didn't always need magic to win a fight.

CHAPTER 12

WHEN SHE AND EMERY arrived at the Parliament building the next day, Ceony protested less vehemently when she was told to sit outside the conference room and wait with Delilah.

"It won't be as long this time," Emery whispered as the others associated with Criminal Affairs filtered into the double-door conference room. His breath against her neck gave her shivers, but she hid them well enough. "For the love of all gods, I hope it's not as long as last time."

He sighed and turned to the conference room, where Mg. Aviosky lingered outside the doors with a frown. This time, however, the expression was directed at Emery. Ceony wondered at that.

The doors closed, and Delilah and Ceony took their seats.

Ceony waited as long as she could stand it—about five minutes—before turning to Delilah. "Let's go. Hurry!"

They scrambled from the foyer to the women's lavatory, passing tired-looking guards. Ceony checked the stalls to ensure the room's vacancy, then secured the deadbolt on the door.

"Did you bring it?" Ceony asked Delilah.

Delilah, who had begun wringing a handkerchief in her small hands, nodded and hurried to the dresser. From behind it, she pulled out a medium-sized frameless oval mirror with only a thin plastic backing. The mirror shined brightly in the light from the chandelier, free of any cracks or tarnishing. Gaffer's glass. It looked barely large enough for Ceony to fit through—just a few inches wider than her shoulders and hips.

Ceony held it carefully in her arms.

"Don't break it, or I won't be able to pull you back," Delilah said. "I had to transport it here late last night after Magician Aviosky went to bed. I thought for sure one of the guards would catch me. Turn it around."

Ceony turned the mirror toward Delilah, who traced it with her finger and synced it with the lavatory mirror. Ceony would take the glider from Emery's cottage to the rendezvous point—she would be a little late—and warp back to Parliament through the oval mirror in her hands. A quick escape, should things get nasty. If all went as planned, she'd have Grath incapacitated and a dozen paper birds flying to alert local police.

Delilah re-enchanted the lavatory mirror, pulling up the image of the cottage's lavatory. She then kissed both of Ceony's cheeks.

"Be quick, and be careful," she whispered. "I swear I'll break my promise and get the magicians involved if you're not back in an hour."

"Give me two," Ceony said. "Just to be safe."

"One and a half, tops," Delilah countered. She took a deep breath. "Go, you stupid girl. And don't get yourself killed!"

Still gripping the oval mirror, Ceony climbed onto the dresser and stepped into the cottage bathroom—a bit of a squeeze, given the height of the bathroom mirror. She stepped down onto the porcelain sink, then leapt to the tiled floor. With everything she needed already prepared and in her bag, she darted from the bathroom, down the hall, and up the stairs to the third floor, where Emery's "big" spells lay, including the glider, a giant paper bird, and some other strange contraption he hadn't yet finished, which she only knew from snooping. No other furniture save for a stool occupied the large, bare-walled space, which was in need of a good sweeping.

After securing a shield chain around her torso, Ceony stood on the glider and pulled the cord that opened the door in the cottage's roof, receiving an angry cry from a raven in the process. Then, situating herself on the glider and gripping its handholds, she said, "Breathe."

The contraption bucked like a wild horse beneath her. Ceony jerked back on the handles, and the glider soared upward through the roof nose first, nearly tossing Ceony from its back. Only after Ceony had straightened it out in the sky, pointing it south, did she realize she would have to return to the cottage to shut the door in the roof. She could only hope it wouldn't rain before then.

Ceony soared toward London far faster than any buggy could take her, freed from the limitations of roads and rivers, and she stayed as far as she could from the rivers. It all looked like one of the elaborate train sets toy stores sold at Christmastime, but with fewer hills and a duller track. She glided westward, preferring to circumvent the city instead of fly directly over it, for she wanted as few witnesses as possible. Wind thrashed her hair, lashing her braid about like a whip. Ceony pressed herself against the glider, urging it to go faster. She only had so much time before Delilah's resolve broke, and she feared it would be less than the agreed-upon hour and a half. She held her breath when she flew over the gray-cast River Thames, but it couldn't be avoided.

Adrenaline didn't start streaming into her blood until she passed London and started searching the ground for Hangman's Road. Her decision suddenly felt very real to her, and her heart beat even louder than the wind rushing by her ears. Her hands began to sweat on the handles of the glider, which she squeezed until her knuckles paled.

Slowing down, Ceony pointed the glider closer to the earth. She veered west, following the line of shallow, green-spotted hills marking a long stretch of abandoned farmland. In the shadows of those hills she spied a rust-colored barn, large enough to house several animals. A spattering of weatherworn holes marked the west side of its seal-colored roof, and one of its white-streaked front doors rested crookedly on its hinges. A collapsed cowshed lay just a few yards to its right.

Coaxing the glider up, she circled the house and hills, searching for anything out of the ordinary, anything to indicate Grath had laid a trap for her. She saw nothing.

"Land gently, please," she begged the glider. She guided it east of the barn. The glider circled three and a half times before skidding on its belly across the long grass.

Ceony flexed her sore hands and slid off the glider, glancing warily at the barn. No sign of Grath. Not yet, anyway.

Reaching into her bag, she unfurled her paper doll. "Stand," she ordered.

The paper doll stiffened and stood. Aligning herself with it, Ceony said, "Copy."

The doll colored itself to match her, wind-mussed hair and all. Ceony didn't bother to smooth it down.

Clutching Delilah's mirror to her chest and the paper doll under one arm, Ceony cautiously approached the barn, stepping as lightly as the untamed land would allow. She peeked in past the crooked door.

Streaks of sunlight filtered into the barn through the holes in the roof. Empty stables built of splintering wood lined two of the walls, which were studded with hooks and loops that had once held tools. A few pieces of old, dry hay lay scattered over a dirt floor. Bird droppings stained the rafters. But what really drew Ceony's attention were all the mirrors.

Dozens of them occupied the wide space, some as small as Delilah's compact, others as tall as the vanity mirror Ceony had shattered. They sat or hung all around the barn, against walls or on the floor, tilted up and down, left and right. Had Grath set these up solely for their meeting, or had he been hiding here the entire time?

Whispering to her paper doll, Ceony left it outside the doors and stepped into the barn, setting her oval mirror against the wall, pleased by how well it blended in with its reflective sisters. Ceony checked the links of her shield chain and reached into her bag, touching each of her spells. She rested her fingers on the barrel of her pistol.

"Grath!" she shouted. "Where—"

"I'm never late for an appointment, sweetheart," his honey-slick voice said. Ceony whirled around, spying him first in a mirror, and then his true, solid-bodied self in the opposite corner, near an old worn-out saddle on the wall. This time he didn't wear his false nose, or clothing common in London fashion—he had donned a black shirt with sleeves so short it was nearly sleeveless, and a black jeweled belt across his torso. No, not jeweled—tiny mirrors dotted the leather. He wore well-fitted black slacks, too, and black boots.

Grath folded his arms, which looked notably larger than Ceony remembered them being. She didn't even think Langston could hold his own against the man. She hoped the bulk was just a trick of the sleeves.

Though Grath wasn't an Excisioner, Ceony still wanted to avoid all physical contact with him. After all, shield chains would only protect her from spells, not a man's hands.

She cleared her throat, hoping to banish the fear from her voice. "Where's Lira?" she asked. She winced at the tremble in her words.

Grath strode forward, and despite Ceony's desire to show bravery, she took several steps back. The Gaffer smiled at her, but made no comment about her cowardice.

He paused by a stall and gestured to one of the larger mirrors at the back of the barn. "See for yourself."

Keeping Grath in her peripheral vision, Ceony sidestepped until she could see into the mirror. Instead of her own reflection, she saw Lira, just as she remembered her.

The dark-haired woman crouched, flakes of frost clinging to her limbs and black clothing. Her face was contorted in a half scream, and one red-stained hand was pressed to her left eye, desperately trying to stanch the blood that dripped down her cheek and forearm. Blood from where Ceony had used Lira's own dagger to defend herself. Small branches of ice glittered off the frozen woman's skin and clothing.

The one thing that didn't match Ceony's memory was Lira's location. She crouched not on water-strewn rocks stained with ocean salt, but on dark, splintered floorboards dotted with mouse droppings. The mirror didn't let in enough light for Ceony to see the rest of the space.

"You didn't bring her here," Ceony said, pulse quickening. She looked back at Grath. "How can I help her if she's not here?"

"Don't be daft," Grath said, scratching the side of his thick neck with his middle finger. "She's on the other side of that mirror. One word from me, and we can step through it. Like a portal. A few words from you, and she'll be whole again, minus an eye."

He growled those last three words, making him seem much more canine than feline.

Ceony glanced back to Lira. Could she break the spell even if she wanted to? Her words at the gulf had been so absolute, and while she had told Grath the magic wasn't anything special, she feared that wasn't true. No Folding spells used blood in their casting, and Ceony had used blood to freeze Lira. Though both logic and Emery had assured her that that didn't make her an Excisioner, she wondered what it meant. Did she actually have some useful information about switching one's designated casting material?

"I may not have been entirely honest with you at the bistro," Ceony said carefully. Knowledge was a powerful thing, and she didn't want to give too much away. "The spell was accidental, but it may have had some crossover possibilities."

Grath's grin widened. "I knew it," he said, stepping forward. Ceony stepped back, keeping space between them. Surprisingly, Grath halted. He wanted Ceony's information as much as she wanted his, if not more. Hopefully he wouldn't do anything to jeopardize that.

"Tell me," he urged.

"It's a spell only I can unravel, since I'm the caster," Ceony said. A lie, though it could be true. She could cease animation on spells Emery had activated, so it was possible that another Folder could manipulate this spell as well. But Grath wasn't a Folder.

"The spell is in her body, obviously," Ceony said, pushing her voice to keep it firm. "Have you not asked Saraj to break it? Excisioners have powers over the body. Powers you don't have."

"*Saraj greatly disliked Lira,*" she remembered Emery saying. Perhaps the Excisioner hadn't tried, then.

Grath ground his teeth together. "We have a spell that can stiffen the body, yes, but the reversal didn't help Lira. This is a different spell."

Ceony picked apart his words. "Not *we*. Saraj."

Grath's expression darkened. "Yes, Saraj. For now. But I know Excision like the back of my hand, Ceony Twill. If you can't break the curse, I will, once blood is my domain. You haven't let my secret slip, have you?"

He stepped forward.

Ceony held her ground, but she fisted her hand in her bag. "I'm not stupid. I know how to keep things to myself," she lied. All of Criminal Affairs now knew Grath's hidden identity as a Gaffer.

Grath paused again, about seven paces from Ceony. He lifted his hands. "It's all in the material," he murmured, studying his own palms. "I've researched for years, and I know that much. A magician's magic is all in the material. Those blasted sealing words are so easily spoken, yet so final."

He hesitated, then scowled, perhaps realizing Ceony was wasting his time. "Tell me what you did!" he barked. "Fix her!"

Ceony jumped at the volume of his voice, which boomed against the rafters and empty walls of the barn. Mirrors quivered under its strength. Swallowing hard, she took a step toward Lira's mirror.

She stared at Lira, the thorny beauty whose hand and hair concealed most of her face as she crouched in unending agony. Emery had loved her, once. Three years he'd been married to her. Even when Lira had turned away from him, even when Grath had pulled her to darkness, Emery had still loved her. Not until the very end—when all hope had been lost—had he severed the bond between them. Ceony knew. She had seen it for herself.

Lira had been a nurse, Emery had said. A healer. Nurses helped people. Perhaps that was what had drawn Emery to her, besides her beauty. Lira had worked to cure the sick.

Ceony's memory swirled to the rocky cave on Foulness Island, where Emery's heart had sat beating in a pool of enchanted blood. Ceony had shot Lira in the chest with her pistol. But the Excisioner had used dark magic to pull the bullet free, healing herself. For a brief moment, under Grath's scrutiny, Ceony wondered if that could have been what drew Lira to Excision. Had Grath offered her a way to heal people to which modern medicine couldn't compare? Had Lira initially wanted to be the kind of person who could heal someone with just a single touch, a single spell?

Ceony peered into the mirror. Lira *had* been a good person, once. To win Emery's love, she must have been. But Excision had darkened her, stolen her soul away.

"Grath was our neighbor when we lived in Berkshire . . ."

Grath. She turned toward him. Grath had planted the evil in Lira's heart, nourished it like a gardener would his plot. No, Ceony wouldn't free Lira; Emery had given her chance after chance, and she had proved she had no redemption left in her.

But Ceony couldn't free Grath, either. She couldn't let him go back to the city and hurt more people, draw more innocents into the dark arts. Possibly become an Excisioner himself. She had to stop it.

Reaching down to the very base of her bag, Ceony gripped her Tatham percussion-lock pistol and pulled it free from its bed of Folded spells.

She leveled it at Grath.

CHAPTER 13

GRATH FROWNED AT THE pistol. "Is this your plan, pet?"

"You're not an Excisioner," she said flatly, though she moved her other hand to the pistol to hold it steady. She hadn't used the gun since her confrontation with Lira, and the rickety barn hardly made for ideal concentration. "You can't heal from it like Lira did."

"Are you so sure?" he asked.

Ceony leveled the gun at his heart.

Grath stepped forward. Ceony cocked the hammer.

He chuckled. "You ever killed someone before, little girl?" he asked.

"I did that, didn't I?" Ceony said, jerking her head toward the mirror that still showcased Lira. *But that isn't death, just magic*, she thought. *If I shoot him, I'll kill him. I'll be a killer just like he is.*

But no, this was different. This was Grath or Ceony, and Ceony thought a bullet to the chest was undoubtedly far more merciful than whatever Grath had planned for her.

Still, she lowered the muzzle down, to his hip. Better to incapacitate him here and let Criminal Affairs deal with him.

She hated how the gun trembled in her grip.

Grath did not seem amused. "I'll track down your blond friend like I promised. Delilah Berget, isn't it?"

Ceony tried very hard not to glance at the oval mirror by the doors.

Reaching behind him, Grath pulled two short daggers from his belt, their blades made of thick, frosted glass. They looked like carved ice. He brought one to his lips and kissed it.

"I'll cut off her toes first," he said, taking a small step forward, sliding his boot across the dirt floor. "Then her fingers, her ears. I'll pull her teeth one by one, then her tongue. And when she can't scream anymore, I'll—"

"Stop it!" Ceony shouted. "It doesn't matter! I'll stop you, and Delilah will be fine!"

"Oh, she might be, but what about the others?" Grath asked. "You don't know much about Saraj, do you? He's a mad dog, the kind that kills for fun, not for food. He'll go after your friend, and Patrice Aviosky, and Emery Thane. He even blew up the Dartford Paper Mill just to flush you out.

"But he won't stop there," he continued. "With him, it's always a game. I already know who's on his list. Ernest John Twill, Rhonda Montgomery Twill . . ."

Every muscle in Ceony's body tensed, distorting her aim. Those were her parents' names.

Grath didn't stop. "Zina Ann, Marshall Ernest, and Margo Penelope. It *is* Penelope, isn't it?"

Ceony's mouth dried to desert. Airy tears stung her eyes. Her hands perspired around the gun. *He knows my family's names. How does he know their names?!*

"Don't you see, pet?" Grath asked, taking another sliding step forward. "I'm Saraj's leash. If something happens to me, he'll be let loose on the world—"

Grath moved so swiftly he blurred, a swathe of peach, black, and light. His blade whistled through the air, and suddenly Ceony's pistol jerked from her clammy hands, hitting the ground some eight paces behind her. One of Grath's daggers landed beside it.

Ceony's heart dropped to her heels. She bolted for the oval mirror.

"Oh no," Grath growled, and his heavy footsteps pursued her like a locomotive, boots smashing into the ground hard enough to shake it. Ceony shrieked and grabbed a handful of spells, throwing them behind her without even stopping to see what they were.

"Breathe!" she cried.

Three paper birds came to life, and one Burst spell fell to the ground, useless.

The birds sailed for Grath, but he pushed through the paper creations without even pausing.

"Delilah!" Ceony screamed as she neared the mirror. Its surface rippled, but Grath's giant hand grabbed Ceony's wrist and yanked her back.

For a quarter of a second Ceony flew, the barn spinning. Then she collided with the dirt, and a cloud of dust swelled up around her, stinging her eyes and coating her tongue. She coughed and pushed herself up, her right shoulder protesting.

Grath picked up the oval mirror. "Cute," he said. "Shatter."

Under the Gaffer's light touch, the mirror broke into hundreds of pieces, falling to the ground like frozen rain. Amid the ringing of so many shards, Ceony heard Delilah scream her name.

Panting, Ceony stared wide-eyed at her ruined means of escape. But she still had the glider. If she could only reach the glider—

Grath switched his dagger to his right hand and charged.

Ceony pulled a paper rhombus from her bag and shouted, "Burst!"

The spell hovered between them, quivering wildly. Ceony ran to the back of the barn before it exploded in a firework of white and yellow. Some of its ashes curled around her, repelled by the shield chain.

Grath had vanished, leaving the path to the doors clear.

Ceony ran, but as she moved, a tall mirror to her right rippled and Grath passed through it. His huge arms swung for her like massive crab claws. Ceony ducked, half-tripping, and kicked him hard in the shin. She scrambled against the loose dirt on the floor and sprinted for the door, leaving the Gaffer cursing behind her.

She had almost reached the doors when another circular mirror rippled, and Grath stepped out. He said something Ceony couldn't hear, and suddenly *every* mirror in the barn rippled. A copy of Grath stepped out from *all* of them. Soon dozens of Grath Cobalts surrounded her, some huge and menacing, some only a few inches high, hovering before the tiny mirrors that lined the wall.

Ceony stepped back, blinking sweat from her eyes. The copies of Grath had a slightly airy look to them, almost like a story illusion. But which one was real? And could the illusions hurt her?

"Don't run, pet," all the Graths said in unison, a songless choir.

She had one Burst spell left. Best to try the Grath closest to the door.

"Burst!" she cried, flinging the spell toward a mirror with an iron-cast frame, the one the first Grath had stepped through. She backtracked and called, "Move!"

The Burst spell exploded, its light reflecting through the enchanted mirrors, incinerating the Gaffer's copies of himself.

Ceony ducked down, and the real Grath emerged from another mirror on the east side of the barn. He threw his dagger right at Ceony—

And it ripped through paper.

Grath, now unarmed, watched with a pale expression as Ceony's paper doll—now torn from nose to collar—lost its color and drifted to the ground. The Mobility spell she'd placed on the doll earlier had brought it into the barn with Ceony's second command.

The real Ceony stood and rushed for the doors, her hand searching for her bag, her eyes whipping between two other mirrors.

Grath transported to the one on the left, but Ceony pulled her Ripple spell free. Grath charged, a human bull.

"Ripple!" Ceony commanded the spell as its jellyfish-like folds cascaded downward.

The air around her warped, not unlike the glass of a mirror before transport. Grath wavered in his charge, but not enough. He reached Ceony, pulled back his right fist, and swung.

A sound like thunder echoed through Ceony's skull, followed by wide streaks of lightning. She landed on the ground hard, the impact jarring up through her tailbone.

Fire burst from her left cheek, just below her eye. The rafters spun around her, this way and that, unsure of their direction.

Then she felt thick fingers ripping the shield chain from her torso. The barn spun harder as one of his hands circled her neck and the other gripped the front of her blouse, hoisting her up. He slammed her against the wall just beside the doors. Splinters dug into her back, and bits of dust sprinkled her shoulders.

Grath held Ceony a few inches above his crown. He squeezed her throat, and Ceony choked for air. He took a second to catch his breath before he said, "Do you know how an Excisioner bonds, Ceony?"

But Ceony couldn't answer. Grath's fingertips pressed into her windpipe. Her face grew hot and her cheek throbbed, drumming into her skull.

"I can't do it yet," he said, "but I can demonstrate well enough." He squeezed harder. Ceony's feet flailed.

The loud clap of a gunshot rang through the barn, and Ceony fell.

She hit the ground on her knees and gasped, hot air filling her lungs. Grath grunted and staggered back, his huge hands flying to his ribs. Blood poured down the side of his shirt—a graze, but it bled a steady stream.

Ceony gaped at Delilah, who stood beside one of the empty stalls, Ceony's pistol gripped in her hands.

"Run!" Delilah cried, and Ceony saw that one of her friend's feet was still inside a rippling mirror. She had found the barn, and just in time.

Ceony jumped to her feet and slammed all her weight into Grath, elbowing his wounded side. The Gaffer staggered back, and Ceony bolted for Delilah.

Delilah slid back through the mirror until only one hand remained above the surface.

"Transport!" Grath shouted from behind her. All the mirrors began again to ripple at once. Grath appeared at the mirror closest to Delilah, still gripping his side, red-faced, breathing hard.

He charged for Ceony.

She wasn't going to make it.

"Run, Delilah!" she cried, darting away from both her friend and Grath.

The mad Gaffer reached for her.

Digging her heel into the ground, Ceony shifted direction, receiving a painful *pop* from her ankle in the process.

She dived through another mirror.

CHAPTER 14

CEONY EXPECTED TO REEMERGE somewhere else in the barn, somewhere that would give her a good shot for the door, but when she tripped out of the mirror frame on the other side, she stumbled into near darkness, the smells of wood and rot assailing her.

This wasn't the barn, but it didn't matter.

Pushing herself up, Ceony grabbed the frame of the rippling mirror and threw it down with all her might, breaking it into several pieces. The rippling ceased, but Ceony jumped on the larger pieces anyway, splitting them beneath the heels of her shoes.

Wincing, she staggered backward, favoring her right leg. Her left ankle throbbed fiercely, almost as badly as her cheekbone did.

She breathed heavy breaths that echoed through the dark emptiness around her and wheezed like October wind. Ceony coughed, then coughed again, her hand flying to her sore throat. A third cough almost made her retch, but her desperation for air kept the contents of her stomach down. She swallowed twice, still watching the mirror. She had no paper for a blind box. She had nothing at all, not even her pistol. Just an empty bag.

"Oh, Delilah," she whispered, hoarse. Surely her friend had gotten away in time.

Another swallow, and Ceony finally lifted her eyes, taking in the shadows around her. The stale air felt cool against her sweating skin. Her eyes adjusted to the darkness, and she saw old, taupe-colored walls made of thin wooden boards, a flat ceiling, a wooden floor strewn with mouse droppings. A storage shed of sorts, perhaps. An empty one.

She turned around. Not empty.

Her quick-beating heart lodged into the base of her raw throat at the sight of Lira, still frozen, crouching with her hands pressed to her face, still locked into the agony into which Ceony had frozen her on the shores of Foulness Island. She looked like a phantom in the shadows of the shed. Ethereal, ghostly. Ceony shivered.

She circumvented Lira, giving her a wide berth, and stepped toward the door, limping on her left side. The floorboards creaked under her weight, setting off the skittering of tiny, clawed feet in the walls, or perhaps underfoot. Mice.

Ceony tested the doors. Locked, but closer inspection told her they hadn't been locked from the outside. Someone—Ceony assumed Grath—had installed two locks on the inside. Both required a key. Ceony's shoulders drooped.

Ceony reeled back toward the remnants of the mirror, which she could barely see this close to the door, where the only light filtered through gaps between the wooden panels of the walls.

Grath. Grath knew where she had gone. He wouldn't trust her here with Lira. He'd come for her, one way or another. Come for her and kill her.

"Oh God, help me," she whispered, clutching both hands to her chest. Her body shivered.

She tested the locks, pulling at them, trying to wedge a fingernail into the screws that held them. They didn't budge.

If only she had paper! A burst spell would blow the decrepit wood apart, surely.

She chewed on her lip, skin growing colder by the minute. She pushed against the doors, the splintering wood creaking with the force. Pushing her fingers through one of the larger gaps, she gripped the board and pushed, pulled, pushed, but she didn't have the strength to break it.

"Think, think," she whispered. No paper. What else did she have?

She glanced toward Lira, hobbled toward her.

The woman's skin felt ice cold, and Ceony half-expected her to reanimate and strike her. The thought of being trapped in a shed with a vengeful Lira made her shudder. Still, she prodded the woman's belt, her pants, her shirt, searching for anything that might be useful. She found a German train ticket that hadn't been stamped and some sort of long nail or stake hooked through a belt loop.

Ceony drew a small switchblade from Lira's right boot, about three inches long. She took that, the nail, a shard of glass, and the broken mirror's frame and returned to the door.

First she tried wedging the nail between lock and wood and pounding it in with the handle of the switchblade, but the lock didn't come loose and the tools slipped in her clammy hands. She wiped her palms on her skirt and tried dislodging the lock with the blade itself, but without success.

Tucking the switchblade into her camisole, Ceony grabbed hold of the mirror frame, careful not to cut her fingers on the remaining shards of glass. She winced as she placed her weight on her left ankle. Then, holding the frame at an angle, she brought her right foot down on it twice before the frame snapped on its long end. Ceony wrenched it back and forth until she had a good, long piece of painted wood in her hands. Heaving with the effort, Ceony shoved the frame end into the gap between the wood panels and worked it back and forth, leaning all her weight into the lever.

The wood creaked, then split at the bottom.

A surge of hope rushed through Ceony, and she dropped the frame and grabbed the wood, ignoring the splinters that dug into her palms and fingers. She pushed it out until it broke again three feet up. Placing her weight on her left foot once again, Ceony kicked at the rest of the board until it loosened and she could bend it out.

The tight fit scraped her shoulder blades and hips, but Ceony pushed out of the storage shed. An identical building stood next to it, both of them situated on a dirt clearing near an unpaved trail. A gray, overcast sky hovered above, and Ceony smelled the distant scents of salt and fish: the coast.

She stumbled away from the sheds, hurrying up the three-foot-wide trail and disappearing into the trees. No memory in her arsenal matched this place. Where was she?

Grath. Her cheek throbbed, neck burned.

It didn't matter where the mirror had taken her. She had to run before he found her.

She took off down the trail at a lope, limping on her left leg. She didn't appear to be on a mountainside, thankfully, just in a patch of untamed woodland filled with mossy fir trees and weeds. After about a quarter mile, she stepped off the trail, scared that Grath would take that path first to find her.

She sprinted as best she could through knee-high foliage, eyes on the ground to avoid tree roots and dips. She ran a ways before stopping and ducking behind a yew tree, her lungs burning, her ankle throbbing. Blinking back tears, Ceony lowered herself to the ground and pulled off her shoe and stocking.

Her ankle certainly wasn't broken, and had only swelled a small amount. A light sprain, perhaps, or just a twist. Nothing that wouldn't cure itself, though she didn't have the option of resting right now.

She pulled her stocking and shoe back on to keep the swelling down, then retrieved the mirror shard from the shed. She cradled it in her hands.

"Find me, Delilah," she whispered. "Come on. You found me before, find me now."

She stared at her own desperate reflection for a good minute, but nothing happened. She hadn't expected anything different.

Ceony leaned back against the tree, trying to catch her breath. She didn't even know where she was, so how would Delilah? If only Ceony were a Gaffer . . .

Memories of Grath's threats filled her mind, and her heart sped with a renewed vigor. Her family. *He's going to hurt my family. Kill them. I have to get back!*

Ceony cursed herself again and again as she stood, leaning against the tree for support. She had to find help. If she could only find some paper, perhaps she could send out a bird to search for Emery—

Emery's going to kill me himself, she thought, hurrying through the scrubby woodland. *I'm going to be expelled from my apprenticeship for sure.*

But that didn't matter, not right now. She had to find help. She had to warn her family. And more pressingly, she had to get away from Grath!

On she ran, more of a lopsided jog, through the woodland. The trees thinned and a few raindrops hit her nose, but the sky remained mostly dry. After a while, the earth slanted down a bit, and the trail turned east. She followed it for several miles until her muscles ached and her throat cried for water.

It ended at a wide, dirt road that went straight in both directions, no houses or signs of life along it save for a weathered sign carved in French.

French. So, she had left England. But where was she? France? Belgium? Certainly Grath wouldn't have carried Lira clear to Canada!

Coughing, Ceony followed the road at little more than a walk. The thick clouds hid the sun, but she could tell the day had stretched into evening.

She looked over her shoulder, thinking she heard movement, but saw nothing.

She searched the sides of the road as she went, hoping to find some discarded trash made of paper, but the grounds were clean. She couldn't even find a stick large enough to use as a cane. The ruts in the road were shallow, barely there. Wherever she had materialized, few people went.

She continued on, a cool breeze chilling her skin, her limp nearly a drag now. Her ankle had swelled more, but she couldn't stop. She had to find someone. She had to get away. If only she could find a telegraph somewhere, but she didn't see any wires. She didn't even find any more signs, not that she could have read them anyway.

As the sun began to set, tinting the overcast clouds orange, she clutched the glass shard in her hands, murmuring Delilah's name, Mg. Aviosky's, Emery's. No one heard her.

She followed the road until night settled too heavily for her to see, and the clouds hid the moon and stars. Panting, Ceony stepped off the road and back into the sparse trees. She sat between the roots of one, pulled her knees to her chest, and wept.

CHAPTER 15

A LIGHT SPRINKLING OF rain and soft gray light woke Ceony early
in the morning, just as the cry of some wild bird and the skittering
of an unseen animal had twice during the night. Her right leg tingled below the knee, and her sore back creaked as she straightened
against the tree trunk. A large brown spider crept down her shoulder;
Ceony shrieked, slapped it off, and jumped to her feet, stumbling
on her dead leg. Her left ankle, at least, seemed much better, and
the swelling had gone down while she slept.

She looked about the tree, trying to organize her scattered
thoughts. Mist clung to her clothes and dripped from heavy leaves
overhead.

Pulling out Lira's switchblade, Ceony scanned the forest,
searching for a flash of ginger hair, or for any sign of human life.
She saw none. Still, if Grath had transported to wherever Ceony
was and tracked back to the shed yesterday, it wouldn't take him
long to find her.

She put the switchblade back into her camisole and examined
her mirror shard, but the glass remained smooth and unenchanted.

Hopefully carrying it with her wouldn't be a two-edged sword, but even if Grath's image appeared in the glass, he wouldn't know how to find her. At least Ceony hoped he wouldn't. This was a shard from *his* mirror, after all.

She climbed back to the road, thinking that if she could find another inhabitant, she could get help. Or at least a piece of paper. Though in this rain, a paper bird wouldn't make it very far.

And Ceony had no idea just how many miles stretched between her and London, or how many bodies of water. Still, she could only go onward.

She followed the road.

The gray sky brightened as she walked, yet the sun refused to break its cloud cover. It rained long enough to make Ceony's clothes feel uncomfortable, then stopped, leaving the world awfully cold for late summer. She unbraided her hair and combed her fingers through it, rebraided it. Checked the mirror. Glanced over her shoulder.

After some time, perhaps two hours, she heard the rattling of carriage wheels on the dirt road ahead of her. A stout, unpainted carriage pulled by two spotted horses came into view. Relieved, Ceony ran toward it, waving her arms to stop the driver, but he ignored her and continued on, quickening the horses' trot as he passed. The carriage windows had their shutters drawn.

Ceony paused in the road, staring after them. A young woman in distress, and they hadn't even slowed? Curse the French! Who did they think she was, and what errand could they possibly have in the middle of nowhere that they couldn't so much as stop to give her directions?

Shoulders slumping, Ceony turned back to the road. She didn't need directions, and wouldn't understand them anyhow. She had only two options: go forward, or return to the shed.

Ceony moved forward at a quicker clip, rubbing a hunger cramp from her stomach as she went. The carriage must have come from somewhere, and the horses didn't look too exhausted. *Only a few more hours*, she thought, hopeful.

The trees thinned even more, and the rain picked up again, sprinkling on and off, defying the warmth of the hidden sun. Ceony rubbed a chill from her fingers as she walked, searching for any hint of life. She spied a wild rabbit and for a moment wished she knew how to hunt the animal, not just how to cook it.

She tried holding her mouth open to the rain for a drink, but the droplets were so fine and temperamental that it did nothing to quench her thirst. She continued walking, her muscles sore, clutching the mirror in her hands. *Find me Delilah, Magician Aviosky. Find me before Grath does.*

She tried not to think of her family, but walking in silence down the never-ending road, the feat proved difficult. She imagined Marshall on the floor in the storage room of the meatpacking warehouse, imagined Zina hanging by one of the hooks, Emery and the constable standing over them. Only this time, all the blame lay on Ceony's shoulders.

Shaking the thoughts away, Ceony peered behind her, thinking for a moment that she heard heavy footsteps, or saw a flash of ginger hair, paler than her own. But no—she was alone. She didn't feel that same uneasy, hair-raising feeling that came upon her whenever Saraj was close.

More time passed and she found another sign, this one reading, "Zuydcoote un kilometre au sud-est." She imagined "kilometre" meant kilometer, but she couldn't piece together the rest. Still, a sign meant civilization had to be nearby. She hoped.

She picked up her pace, her stomach growling audibly now, and to her relief, she saw a cultivated hill covered in trimmed crabgrass and a small redbrick house atop it, off the road a ways. Finding a new ball of energy inside her, Ceony ran across the road and up the hill, not bothering to look for a pathway. She reached the narrow porch, breathless, and knocked on the door that bore a faded sign reading "Claes."

She heard creaking footsteps beyond the door, and then a balding man who looked to be in his late forties answered the door.

"Hello, I'm so sorry," Ceony blurted, "but I'm lost and I need help. Do you have a telegraph?"

The man crossed his brows. "Et, qui êtes-vous? Je ne parle pas l'anglais."

Oh, how she wished Delilah were here to translate! Ceony's grip tightened on the mirror, but with her free hand she pointed to herself and said, "Ceony. Lost. From England."

She pointed in what she assumed was the direction of England. Then an idea struck her.

She tucked the mirror shard into her waistband and pretended to write on her hand. "Paper?" she asked. "Uh . . . papel? Papier? See-voo play?"

She thought that sounded French.

He paused, then nodded and opened the door, motioning with one hand for Ceony to enter. A slightly older man who resembled the first sat on a short, apricot-colored couch with a newspaper on his lap. He eyed Ceony with curiosity.

The first man moved to a desk in the corner of the room and pulled out a small pad of paper and a pencil. "Papier?" he asked, holding out the supplies.

"Yes, yes! Uh, *oui*," Ceony said, grasping the pad. The familiar tingle of the paper beneath her fingers gave her some comfort. She quickly scribbled a sentence on the first page, receiving strange looks from both men. When she had finished, she read, with strong inflection, "After losing her way through mirror transportation, Ceony found herself in an unfamiliar place and unsure of how to get home."

She pictured what images would best illustrate her point, and they danced before her in the air—ghostly, translucent pictures of what happened to get her to this house. The two men jumped a little when the images first appeared, but then they watched in fascination.

She lowered the pad and wrote some more, then read, "Ceony wondered where she was."

The image of a map of Europe floated before her, with a question mark hovering above it and a thumbtack wavering between England and France.

"Belgique," the first man said. He hesitated, glancing at the man who Ceony assumed was his brother. In a poor English accent, he said, "Belgium."

"Belgium?" Ceony repeated, and the story illusion dripped away like wet paint. *And I smelled the ocean . . . That must have been the English Channel. I crossed it through the mirror.*

How on earth would she get back?

"Gaffer?" she asked, drawing a stick figure below her words and sketching a hand mirror in its hands. "Do you have a Gaffer here?" She lowered the pad and stepped over to the window, tapping on the glass.

The first man turned to his brother and said, "Je pense qu'elle est celle qu'il veut. Elle est rousse. Elle enchante papier."

"Papier," Ceony repeated, nodding. At least she knew that word. "Oui, papier."

The brother nodded, and the first man gestured for Ceony to follow him farther into the house. He held out his hands, and she reluctantly handed over the pad. Perhaps the generosity of these men would extend to offering her a quick meal, too. Her stomach growled. She hoped the man heard it.

If he did, he didn't show it.

Ceony followed him through a small but immaculate kitchen, then down a steep set of stairs that required her guide to hunch over to keep his head from hitting the ceiling. In the basement she passed a closed door; then the man led her into an empty, rectangular room with a few crates stacked in the corner. Near the crates, an old mirror with a broken frame leaned against the wall.

Ceony froze just inside the door. Behind the mirror, arms folded across his broad chest, stood Grath Cobalt.

"Est-ce que c'est la fille? On a le douxieme parti?" the man asked, barring the door with his arm when Ceony tried to back away.

"Bien sûr, vous avez bien fait," Grath answered in a flawless French accent, his gray eyes focusing on Ceony, whose heart had begun to beat so high in her throat she could almost taste it. "S'il vous plaît, donnez-moi un instant."

The man nodded and stepped out of the room, shutting the door behind him.

Ceony reached for the handle.

"Nuh-uh," Grath said, unfolding his arms. "I'm used to wild goose chases, love, but I'm much better when I play the goose." He took a step forward. "For us, this ends now."

Ceony trembled. "P-Please, I don't have what you want," she murmured. "Just let me go."

"And risk more scars?" he asked, rubbing his side where Delilah had shot him. His shirt still bore a hole from the bullet, but the skin underneath looked unscathed. Had Grath visited Saraj before tracking her down? Did that mean the Excisioner still lurked in the city, or did Grath just know how to find him using the mirrors?

Ceony seized the door handle, only to find it locked. She hadn't even heard the metal click.

Her stomach sank, no longer hungry. Tears sprang to her eyes. "I'll d-do whatever you want," she whispered. "Her blood spilled on my paper. It was an Illusion spell, but I wrote the words in her blood, and it took. That's all I did. Please don't hurt my family."

Grath took another step forward, and another, his face a mask that her words didn't alter. Ceony focused so intently on him—on the vein throbbing in his forehead and the shadows dancing in his eyes—that she didn't notice the swirling mirror behind him. One moment, Grath was sauntering toward her, and the next a familiar voice called out to him from behind, freezing him in his tracks.

"We really should stop meeting like this."

A surge of relief rushed through Ceony with such force she nearly lost her balance. Grath scowled and turned, one shoulder still pointed toward Ceony.

There, on the right side of the mirror, stood Emery without his indigo coat. His features looked sharper, darker. His voice lacked its usual mirth. On the left side of the mirror stood Mg. Hughes, who looked rather calm given the situation.

The mirror still swirled, but Ceony didn't need to see through it to know who had enchanted it, who had found her. *Magician Aviosky. Thank God.*

Mg. Hughes said, "Sorry for the delay, Miss Twill, but bad glass is incredibly hard to pass through, once it's found."

Two tears traced the curve of Ceony's cheeks. "Thank you," she breathed.

Emery's eyes focused on Grath. He held his left hand in his pocket, perhaps holding a spell there. Mg. Hughes conspicuously kneaded three small rubber balls in his right hand.

Grath straightened, his confidence boosted. "Such annoying timing, Thane," he said. "I was almost done here."

Mg. Hughes lifted his hand, drawing Grath's attention. The man tensed, ready for a spell, but instead Emery's hand whipped out of his slacks and tossed blue confetti into the air, so many tiny shreds of paper that, for a moment, it concealed him completely.

And then he vanished.

A moment later, Ceony felt a hand on her waist as Emery pushed her behind him. He too tried the door, but of course found it locked.

"We need another mirror, Patrice!" Emery shouted.

Grath laughed, taking two steps back so he could see both magicians clearly. He even clapped his hands twice. "What a show, what a show," he laughed. "Three against one, and yet for some reason I still feel I have the upper hand."

"Grath—" Ceony began, but Emery shushed her.

"We don't negotiate with criminals, Miss Twill," Mg. Hughes said, still kneading those balls. "I'll hang you by the rubber in your shoes, Cobalt."

"Hmm," Grath said, rubbing his chin. "But what do you want, old man? Me, or the girl? I don't see how you'll get out of here with both, plus your life."

From the swirling mirror, Aviosky's disjointed voice said, "There's a decent-sized mirror in a lavatory upstairs."

Grath frowned. "It just takes one touch, Alfred."

Mg. Hughes laughed. "We know what you are. Don't play us for fools."

Grath scowled, and Ceony knew that the expression was meant for her.

After a moment, Grath did turn, slowly, to face Emery. He pulled one of his glass knives from his belt and thumbed the blade, looking the paper magician up and down. "You won't win, in the end," Grath said, one of his long canines popping over his lip as he smirked. "You never do. Not with me, not with Saraj. Not with Lira. She was my finest acquisition."

Emery said nothing.

Grath's eyes slid over Emery's shoulder for a second, and he leered at Ceony. "So protective. I should have had my way with her, too."

Emery tensed. "I'll see they cut your tongue out before you get the noose, Grath."

Grath lifted his blade, but Mg. Hughes moved faster.

He threw the rubber balls, which bounced off the floor and soared in three different directions at an alarming speed, catapulting off walls and ceiling, blurring into bullets of black. They orbited around Mg. Hughes, Emery, and Ceony, but not Grath. One skinned his shoulder, leaving a wide streak of red in its wake. They forced Grath to dance and dodge to avoid being shot through.

Ceony didn't have a chance to witness Grath's counterattack. Emery pulled her away from the door and slammed his foot into the wood, just beside the knob. The weak lock gave and the door flew open, slamming into the wall beside it. With an almost painful grip on Ceony's forearm, Emery yanked her from the room and up the stairs, into the kitchen. The man who had answered the door started from near the sink. Emery elbowed him out of the way and ran through the kitchen and into the hallway. He opened one door to a bedroom, then another to the lavatory, where a mirror about three feet by two rested lopsided on a white cabinet with chipped paint. Its silvery face swirled with a Transport spell.

After releasing Ceony, Emery wrenched the mirror from the wall and set it on the floor, then grabbed her by the shoulders and pushed her into it. Ceony's stomach lurched as a cold weightlessness overtook her, but she didn't reemerge in the Parliament building. She didn't pass through the mirror at all.

She stood inside of it, surrounded by swirling silver walls that warped in shape between concave and convex. Before her hovered a floating silver rock, darker than the walls, and to her right a few stalagmites jutted up from the silvery ground like teeth. A solid-looking cloud hovered a ways ahead, and Ceony realized it was the physical form of a scratch on the mirror.

Delilah had warned her about passing through bad mirrors. This must have been what she meant.

Emery appeared beside her a moment later. He cursed softly, then once more took Ceony's arm. "Stay close," he said.

He led her along the stalagmites toward the hovering boulder—a chip, perhaps, or a tarnish. They ducked under it, careful not to lift their heads until they'd passed it completely. When they reached the vertical cloud, which resembled a spiderweb of glass, menacing and sharp, Emery pulled Ceony to the right. They sidestepped until they had circled the farthest stretches of its web.

Another wall faced them, swirling and bright. Emery nudged Ceony forward, and she passed through its cold embrace.

CHAPTER 16

IT TOOK CEONY A moment to absorb her surroundings; then she realized she was in the small rectangular mirror room on the third floor of Mg. Aviosky's house. Muted sunlight poured through the large, multipaned windows to her left, reflecting off dozens of mirrors made of pure Gaffer's glass, all set along the walls in a carefully chosen order. The mirrors were in all different frames and sizes, and one even had notes written along its top corners in Delilah's handwriting. An old book titled *The Shaping of Enchanted Vases for Intermediate Blowing* rested spine-up on the floor, one-third read.

A pair of hands seized Ceony's shoulders, and Delilah's voice snatched her from her daze.

"Oh, Ceony!" she cried, hauling her up with surprising strength. Tears rimmed Delilah's eyes and her usually perfect hair looked a fright. The Gaffer apprentice embraced Ceony tightly. "I thought you were dead! I was so scared!"

"We all were," Mg. Aviosky said from beside her, albeit with considerably less jubilation. Her hand remained affixed to a tall, upright mirror, which swirled beneath her touch.

Ceony turned in Delilah's embrace. "Emery," she whispered, but just as she spoke his name the paper magician emerged from the glimmering whirlpool, his hands clasped to one of Mg. Hughes's forearms. The Siper looked dazed, but Ceony saw no injuries.

Mg. Hughes stumbled over the mirror frame and leaned on Emery to steady himself.

As soon as they were both across, Mg. Aviosky's hand flew from the mirror, returning its surface to normal. She braced Mg. Hughes on the other side.

"Are you all right?" she asked.

Mg. Hughes nodded. "Just fine, but he used a Flash spell on me, and I'm still seeing spots."

Delilah whispered to Ceony, "That's when you increase the amount of light reflected off a glass surface. It works especially well with mirrors, and with enough light it can be blinding."

Mg. Aviosky overheard and frowned. "But not in this case," she said, guiding Mg. Hughes to a chair in the back corner of the room. "It will wear off."

"I've been on the receiving end of spells far worse than this one, Patrice." Mg. Hughes laughed. "I'll be fine after some good blinking."

"A-And Grath?" Ceony asked. She glanced at Emery, but such fire burned in his green eyes that she quickly redirected her gaze to Mg. Hughes.

He rubbed his eyes. "He got away, unfortunately. But I couldn't have expected otherwise. We have men headed to that barn outside London, but I haven't heard from them, good or ill."

Ceony's stomach dropped.

Clearly sensing her change in mood, Delilah cried, "I had to tell them, Ceony! Please don't be angry."

"And it's a good thing!" Mg. Aviosky added, somehow managing to purse her thin lips and scold at the same time. "Good heavens, Miss Twill. It took us all night and most of the day to find you. I'd hate to think what would have happened had luck not been on my side!"

"Indeed," Emery said, almost coldly. He picked up his indigo coat from where it hung over another mirror and draped it over his arm.

"I'm sorry," Ceony whispered, wishing she had a shell like a hermit crab that she could crawl into. She pulled the mirror shard from her waistband and handed it to Mg. Aviosky. "This is from the mirror I came through, in the shed where Grath is keeping Lira."

Mg. Aviosky took the shard. "Perhaps it will be of some use."

"Sounds like it to me," Mg. Hughes said, leaning forward in his chair. He blinked a few more times. "You should join Criminal Affairs, Ceony. You went on a fool's errand and sent us on a wild goose chase, but we got some excellent information from all of your meddling—"

Ceony's eyes widened, and if not for Delilah's arms, she would have staggered. "My family!" she cried. She pulled away from her friend's grasp and turned her gaze to Emery. "Grath said he would target my family, that Saraj would! He knew all their names, Emery!"

Emery's countenance fell. He looked at Mg. Hughes.

The Siper stood from his chair and straightened his vest. "I worried such a threat would arise. It always does, with these types." He rubbed his half beard in thought. "We'll have to see that arrangements are made for the Twills."

"Please, and quickly," Ceony pleaded. "Thank you so much for coming after me, but it's them I'm worried about. Marshall and Margo, they're just kids, and my parents don't have anywhere to go—"

Mg. Hughes, addressing Mg. Aviosky, said, "I'll use your telegraph if I may."

The Gaffer nodded.

Emery stepped away from the others and took Ceony firmly by the upper arm. "Come," he said, hushed.

But before he could pull her from the room, Mg. Aviosky said, "I'd like to speak with both Miss Twill and Delilah before you take her anywhere, Magician Thane. There is a *severe* matter of—"

"My apologies, Patrice," Emery said, quiet but sharp, "but Ceony is *my* apprentice, and *I* will deal with her side of the situation."

With that he tugged Ceony from the mirror room and down the stairs to the second floor, where he opened the lavatory door and pulled her inside, only then releasing her.

She backed up to the footed tub, heart hammering. Emery turned on the electric light and shut the door.

Wiping tears from her eyes, Ceony said, "Emery, I'm—"

"Sorry?" he asked, the word snapping from his mouth. "You're *sorry*? Damn it, Ceony, you could have been killed!"

"You don't think I know that?" she asked.

"No, I don't think you know that," he countered, "or you wouldn't have undertaken such an idiotic endeavor! This is *Grath Cobalt*! Not some pickpocket off the street!"

Ceony started. Other than in the third chamber of his heart, Emery had never shouted at her before.

"What if Saraj had been there?" he asked, his green eyes blazing. "You would be on a meat hook right now, while the rest of us would still be wondering where the hell you disappeared to!"

"Delilah was—"

"And how *dare* you bring Delilah into this!" he interrupted. "Do you realize how mirror transportation works? He could have killed you, then her!"

"I know how it works, I'm not stupid!" Ceony shouted back. "I didn't go into this blind! This is *my* responsibility—they're after *me*—and yet I'm not even allowed to sit in on the meetings discussing it! I thought I should take care of it on my own."

"You thought wrong," Emery said. He ran a hand back through his hair, looking ready to tug it from his scalp. "You have a great deal of good fortune in your blood, Ceony, but you *cannot* continue to take these kinds of risks. You're not immortal. Do you have any idea what it does to me when you put yourself in danger? And so willingly, no less!"

"If I didn't take risks like this, you'd be dead!" she shot back. She swung her hand out, nearly knocking a seashell from the sink beside her. "I can't sit idly by while the rest of the world goes on without me!"

"You do not hold up the world," Emery replied, closer to his normal volume. "You are not God, and it's time you stopped acting like you were."

"You don't even believe in God," Ceony quipped, folding her arms. A sore lump formed in her throat, and tears threatened her eyes. She stared at a spot on the floor, trying to bury the sensations.

"It doesn't matter what I believe, or what you believe, or what anyone in this damn country believes," Emery said. He let out a long breath. "I don't understand you, Ceony. I don't understand why you would do something like this without even telling me. Do you not trust me?"

She lifted her eyes. Beneath the anger in his face, she saw genuine hurt in his eyes.

Her shoulders slumped. "I trust you. You know I trust you. But I don't want to see you hurt, not again. Grath threatened you, too."

"Threats are only threats," Emery said. "If I had a pound for every threat someone has thrown my way, empty or not, I could retire."

He reached up and touched Ceony's cheek. She winced. The spot where Grath had struck her still felt swollen and tender.

"This is not a threat," Emery said, much quieter now. "I know Grath far better than you do, and I know he keeps his promises. You saved my life; now you have to let me save yours. I couldn't fight

Lira, but I *can* fight Grath and Saraj. You have to understand that they're *nothing* like Lira. She was a novice. You're comparing a house pup to wolves."

The tears finally broke through Ceony's resolve and traced uneven lines down her face, wetting Emery's thumb. "It's my fault," she whispered. "Because of me my family is in danger. Oh God, he'll kill them . . ."

Emery dropped his hand to Ceony's shoulder and pulled her toward him. He embraced her, gently. He smelled like charcoal and brown sugar, as though bits of the cottage still clung to him. His shirt collar absorbed Ceony's tears.

"I promise I'll do everything I can to protect your family," he said. "We'll pray it's a bluff. But Grath and Saraj are my business now."

He released her, taking his warmth with him, and opened the door, vanishing back into the hallway.

Ceony stood like a statue for a long moment, numb and broken, feeling cracks form over her heart. Then she shook her head and spun around, following in the wake of the paper magician.

She saw Mg. Aviosky and Delilah first, coming down the stairs from the mirror room.

"I'm putting you on parole, Miss Twill," Mg. Aviosky said, folding her arms tightly across her chest. Beside her, Delilah stared at the floor, digging the toe of her shoe into an eyespot in the wooden boards. "Unfortunately I can't initiate a house arrest, given the circumstances, but should you act out again I will have to consider a dismissal of your apprenticeship."

Ceony felt as though she had shrunk to a foot tall. She swallowed any argument in her throat and said, "That's fair. I'm so sorry. Delilah, I didn't mean for this to happen."

Delilah only shrugged. "We're all chipper now, aren't we?" she asked, but her tone was all melancholy.

She pushed by the two Gaffers, but only made it one step down the stairs leading to the front door before Mg. Aviosky asked, "And where are you going?"

"To find Emery," she said, not caring that it was his first name that formed on her lips. Mg. Aviosky's frown couldn't deepen any further anyway.

She took the stairs quickly, but thankfully her ankle held up well. She peered into the front room, then followed the hallway toward the dining room. She heard Emery's voice and followed it to a small sitting room at the far end of the first floor, passing Mg. Hughes, who was still tapping away at the telegraph near the kitchen.

She found Emery at an antique desk with a telephone piece pressed to his ear.

She caught the end of his conversation. "—out front. Yes. Thank you."

He hung up.

"What are you going to do?" she asked. "You can't just tell me Grath and Saraj are your problem and expect me to be content with that."

"You have no say in the matter," Emery said, keeping his voice low. "And the decision is not only mine."

He walked past her, heading for the front door.

"I have no say in the matter?" Ceony repeated, catching up to him. "You're just going to keep me in the dark, after all this?"

Emery laughed, a mirthless sound. He stopped walking. "I wish I could keep you in the dark," he said, cool and blunt. He kept his voice low to prevent Mg. Hughes from overhearing. "But you won't stay there. I could plead with you on my hands and knees and you still wouldn't stay there, Ceony. You're a candle that won't be snuffed, and now the darkest parts of this world can see you. And they don't tolerate the light."

He shook his head and continued walking. Ceony followed him into the hallway.

"I said I was sorry," she said, the words shaking in her throat. "I'm so sorry, Emery. Please don't be angry with me. If I could go back in time and change it, I would."

"It's unfortunate that time is not a material," he said, pausing just long enough to open the front door. He stepped out into the afternoon light, searching the street beyond the short front yard. He folded his arms. "And I *am* angry with you. I am so"—he paused—"*so* angry with you. But I will take care of you, Ceony. I swear my life on it. I will take care of you."

Ceony's heart twisted in her chest. Gooseflesh prickled her arms, despite the heat. Her gaze dropped to her feet, and all she could think to say was, again, "I'm sorry."

Minutes later an automobile pulled up to the curb and Emery walked toward it. It had no passengers, but when the driver stepped out, Ceony recognized him immediately.

"Langston," she said.

Emery said, "Thank you, for doing this."

"It's not a problem," Langston replied.

Emery turned to Ceony. "You're going to stay with Langston for a little while. He'll see that you have everything you need."

Ceony's jaw fell. "I . . . you're transferring me?"

Langston said, "It's only temporary, until things clear up. I promise you'll be safe. I keep a good watch."

But Ceony shook her head. "I-I don't want to be safe." To Emery, she said, "I want to stay with you."

Emery avoided her gaze. "Take care of her. I'll try not to take too long."

"Take too long?" Ceony repeated. She grabbed Emery's shirt-sleeve. "What exactly are you going to do?"

"Please, Ceony," he said, just a murmur. "Please do this for me. If nothing else, please just get into the auto."

Ceony retracted her hand, feeling as though Emery had slapped her. Her cheek throbbed anew. Unable to bring up words, she merely nodded, and Langston opened the passenger-side door.

Emery turned back to the house without a good-bye. Ceony stared at its doors as Langston drove away, but he never reemerged.

CHAPTER 17

LANGSTON ASKED CEONY SIMPLE questions as they drove, just as he had after rescuing her from the city after the incident at the bistro. But Ceony only stared out the window, watching buildings as they passed, unable to find a drop of conversation in her. After a few blocks, Langston started chatting about the weather and the university library, which had recently accumulated a large collection of American newspapers, which he claimed to be "more honest" than the British ones.

Ceony pressed up against the window as the automobile passed the street she would have turned onto to get to the Mill Squats in Whitechapel, where her family lived. Her father would be at work right now, her mother preparing dinner, her sister Zina out with friends, trying to use up as much free time as possible before the school year began. Marshall would likely be curled up on the couch with a book, and Margo would be outside playing in the dirt, searching for worms or building castles.

Outside, where anyone could see her. Ceony had to warn them.

"Could you take me to the Mill Squats, please?" Ceony pleaded as Langston stopped for a woman crossing the street.

"I'm sorry," Langston replied, and he really did look sorry. He also looked like he wanted to put a padlock on the passenger-side door. "Magician Thane asked me to take you straight home. Are you worried about your family?"

Ceony sank into the seat. "Yes."

"They'll be safe," Langston said, guiding the automobile forward. "Magician Thane is thorough, and if Criminal Affairs is involved, they're probably already at the house, getting things in order."

Ceony nodded, but the young Folder's words could only comfort her so much. They were a threadbare blanket against a winter storm. No matter how tightly Ceony wrapped it around herself, she could do nothing about the holes.

Langston drove down a street not too far from the Parliament building, one lined with town houses on one side and vanity stores on the other. The town houses—tan, white, gray, even salmon pink—all stood five stories tall, and all pressed up one against another so that not even an ant could wriggle its way between them. Langston parked in front of a coffee-brown town house trimmed with black and came around the automobile to let Ceony out. He offered his elbow, but she shook her head and followed him inside on her own.

Langston lived on the second floor, and the interior of his home surprised Ceony, though she couldn't explain why. He had a large living room that bled into a small dining room, all with a wooden floor coated in a shiny, walnut polish. Electric lights hung from the ceiling in single-tiered chandeliers, and wide windows framed by cream-colored curtains added more brightness. The living room had a fainting couch, a wicker chair, and an upright pianoforte. A simple, half-filled bookshelf occupied the wall where the dining room started, and the dining room was equipped with a well-crafted wooden table and six chairs. Around the corner one way was a small kitchen, and around the corner the other way stretched a winding set of stairs to the second floor.

It all looked very clean, very tidy . . . and, compared to Emery's crowded cottage, somewhat sparse. That had to be it, then. Ceony had grown so accustomed to Emery, who used every last inch of space in his home for knickknacks and pointless décor, that Langston's town house felt empty. It felt temporary. And for her, it was, or so she hoped.

Langston showed her upstairs to the guest bedroom, which measured twice the size of her room at the cottage. It had a large square window with a wide sill on the far wall, a closet cut into the closest wall, a short nightstand painted with purple lilies around the edges, and a bed wide enough for three people.

"There's a lavatory down the hall, and there are some clothes in the closet," he said, gesturing to it. "My sister stayed with me a few weeks ago and left some things behind. She's about your size, maybe a little bigger. You're welcome to try them on."

"Thank you," Ceony managed. She tugged uneasily at her right index finger, receiving a quiet *pop* in return.

Langston searched for something else to say, but seemed at a loss for words.

"Could I at least get my dog?" Ceony asked. "I left him at the flat—"

"I really am sorry," Langston said, "but you need to stay here. It won't be for long, I promise."

Ceony nodded, and Langston stepped out of the room.

As soon as she was alone, Ceony walked over to the window, but despite the warmth of the room, she didn't open it. She looked out onto the city, from the small trees planted along the road to the women in posh hats and men chatting over cigars. They all seemed so happy. So oblivious.

Sighing, she slumped to her knees, resting her elbows and chin on the windowsill. Emery still harbored hard feelings toward her, and he had every right. Delilah did, too. And Mg. Aviosky. Only Mg. Hughes had commended her for her stupidity, and his compliments only rubbed salt into burns. Her mind spun, trying to sort out how to make amends, but she found no answers. Nothing better than apologies, which had done her no good so far.

Langston knocked on the door. "Here, this will help with that bruise," he said. He handed her a bag filled with confetti, much like the confetti Emery kept in his icebox. The bag felt cold beneath Ceony's fingers.

"Thank you," she said. Langston departed with a nod, and Ceony pressed the bag to her cheek, wincing at the soreness beneath her skin. She must look dreadful.

She thought about cooking something, if only to thank Langston for his patience, but she found herself without the motivation. Langston, being a sweet man, did bring her some biscuits and honey at a quarter past six. She ate slowly, and not much at all. Her stomach felt too tight, despite her long stint without food, though she did guzzle the glass of water he brought with the biscuits. She chewed almost mechanically, thinking of her family and Delilah. Thinking of Emery.

She stayed up until midnight and slept only in fits, her mind cycling between Grath's threats and her shadowy memories of Saraj from the paper mill, the night of the buggy crash, and the market.

She thought about Grath's words: "*It's all in the material . . . Those blasted sealing words . . .*"

But no one could break a bond, Ceony knew. That had been drilled into her at Tagis Praff, for choosing a material—those who had the option of choosing, at least—was a critical and final decision in the career of a magician. Somewhere in the timeline of his life,

Grath had bonded to glass without proper authority—a felony in and of itself—and that bond couldn't be revoked.

When Ceony finally fell asleep, she dreamed of mirrors, of Emery, and of Grath, on and off, until the rising sun finally gave her an excuse to get out of bed.

———

The next morning Ceony did find a pale-blue blouse that fit. Most of the skirts were both too wide and too long to sit comfortably on her, but she found a light-gray one in the back of the closet that fell to midcalf—shorter than what Ceony typically preferred. It must have been only knee-length on Langston's sister, which made Ceony believe she had to belong to the Liberal Party, for no conservative woman would show so much leg, stockings or no. But Ceony's own skirt had been terribly soiled, so she pulled on the new skirt and used a hairpin to tighten the waistband in the back. She combed out her hair, but without any spare pins or barrettes, she could only braid it over her shoulder.

Downstairs she found Langston eating a bowl of plain oatmeal at the dining table and reading an article in the science section of the newspaper titled "Polymaker Invents Cake-like 'Polystyrene' Plastic, Unsure How to Enchant." He glanced up when Ceony approached, and thoroughly wiped his mouth.

"Have you heard from him?" Ceony asked.

Langston shook his head. "I'm afraid not. Can I get you some breakfast?"

Ceony glanced at the oatmeal—which looked overcooked—and said, "I could cook something, if you'd like. I don't mind. What do you have?"

Langston stared at her dumbfounded for a moment. "Uh . . . well, there's flour in the cupboard."

Ceony managed a genuine smile. "I'll do some exploring."

She rummaged through the kitchen, pleased to see that Langston owned a full-sized stove. The man had mismatched ingredients, but Ceony whipped together some fried tomatoes, salted mushrooms, poached eggs, and some black pudding, albeit not her best batch of it. Langston didn't seem to notice—he thought the tomatoes alone were a treat, and Ceony determined the man needed to get married right away. She wondered if Delilah could be coerced into dating him. She kept the thoughts to herself.

"So," Ceony said when they had finished eating and silence had settled in. She pinched the fabric of her skirt in her fingers, trying to slide it down her legs—not that the Folder could see them, what with the table and all. "What have you been working on? That meeting you said got cancelled . . ."

He glanced up from the newspaper.

"When I first met you," she finished.

He thought for a moment, then straightened. "Oh yes, I recall. It was a meeting with Sinad Mueller and the Praff Academic Board, actually. We rescheduled it for the following day."

Ceony nodded, trying not to frown at the mention of Sinad Mueller. His name was attached to the most prestigious scholarship one could win for the Tagis Praff School for the Magically Inclined, the very scholarship Ceony had lost after dumping a pitcher of very expensive wine on the man's lap. He'd deserved it, after trying to get a hand up her skirt. One of many reasons Ceony preferred her skirts long.

She tugged on the fabric again. "For the scholarship?"

Langston shook his head in the negative. "Oh no, just for the academic schedule. Tagis Praff is considering adding a Folding class to its second-semester courses to spur interest in paper-based magic. The shortage, and all."

"A required class?" Ceony asked. The workload at Tagis Praff had been nearly suffocating during her year there. Surely they wouldn't add more to the curriculum!

"Well," Langston began, playing with the corner of his newspaper, "I think it would do better as an extracurricular course without a grading system—something for interested students to enroll in, should they choose. But Professor Mueller thinks they won't attend unless it's a required class, or for extra credit."

"And you would teach it?"

"Supposedly," Langston said. "Or perhaps we could make it an assembly of sorts, a career day, maybe. I'd only be showing basic craft, something to spike interest—animation, fortune charms, starlights, those sorts of things."

Ceony released her skirt. "Starlights?"

"You don't know them?" Langston asked. "Well, they're small, almost plush-looking stars that light up. Quite nice for birthday parties or power outages. We get those a lot in the city."

Ceony grinned. Margo would love something like that! "Could you show me, please?"

"Uh . . . well, certainly. I could use the practice."

He looked at his newspaper for a moment, considering it, but ultimately stood from the table and moved to the desk in the living room, which held several stacks of paper. He selected some rectangular sheets in yellow and pink and a pair of scissors, and returned to the table.

"Well, you cut a strip," he said, slicing off the long side of a yellow piece of paper.

"Does the size matter?"

"Uh . . . no, I don't think so," he said, finishing his strip. "And then you make a dog-ear Fold . . . Do you know a dog-ear Fold yet?"

"Just make them," Ceony said, "and I'll watch."

Langston nodded, seeming relieved, and proceeded to Fold the star, his stubby fingers creasing the Folds well. He Folded part of the strip into a sort of knot, but didn't give the Folds a hard crease. He formed a small pentagon, wrapping the remaining paper around it like a bandage and tucking in the end to leave the shape clean. He then, carefully, and with his smallest fingers, pressed in each side of the pentagon until it formed a star.

He held the starlight in his hand and said, "Glow."

As though he had lit a match within the paper, the star began to softly glow from within. Ceony had to cup her hands around it to see, what with the bright morning light, but the soft light of the star remained steady until Langston said, "Cease."

"Charming," Ceony said. "I'd like to try, if you don't mind."

Ceony cut a strip and copied Langston's movements from memory, though she had to pause twice to ask questions about the steps Langston's large hands had obscured during the Folding process. When she had finished, she held a small, softly gleaming pink star in her hands. So simple, yet beautiful.

"This would make a wonderful necklace, were it not so fragile," she commented. She wondered if the starlight would still glow if she glossed it the way Emery had glossed her barrette.

Thoughts of Emery dulled her cheer, and she ordered the star, "Cease."

Langston shifted in his chair.

"Do you have any firearms?" Ceony asked, setting the star down. In secondary school, when she had been upset over something, sometimes her father would take her into the countryside to shoot off his shotgun. The pull and thunder always helped empty her mind.

Langston paled. "I . . . well, I'm not supposed to let you out of the house, you see, and you can't use one in here." He rubbed the back of his neck. "I'm not good with lessons—not yet anyway—but

I have some books you could read. Perhaps you'll discover something else Magician Thane hasn't taught you."

"Perhaps," Ceony agreed, slouching in her chair. "I'll browse for myself, if you don't mind."

"Of course."

Pushing back from the table, Ceony collected the dishes, washed them in silence, and picked through books until she found not a textbook, but a copy of *Jane Eyre*. When Langston wasn't looking, she snatched a sheet of paper and a pen from the top of his desk and retired to the guestroom upstairs.

Sitting on her bed and leaning against the novel, Ceony wrote on the paper, *I need you to trust me and leave the house. Go anywhere, take a vacation. I'll send you the money. Please hurry.*

She reread her words and chewed on her bottom lip. For all she knew, Criminal Affairs had yet to take action, or they had decided to use her family as bait to draw out Grath and Saraj. The idea made her stomach churn.

It wouldn't take long for the men to follow through on their threats. And for Saraj, all it would take was one touch.

She thought of the buggy driver and shivered. She slinked down to the floor and Folded the paper against it until she had formed a paper crane.

"Breathe," she said.

The paper bird stretched out its wings and lifted its triangular head to her.

She recited her address to it.

"If no one is home, come straight back here so I know," she said.

The bird bobbed in her hand. Ceony opened her window just wide enough to slip the bird out. It launched over the street below, its white body shrinking out of sight as it flew over the next row of town houses.

Ceony sighed and closed the window. She hated not knowing.

Leaning on the sill, she peered down to the street lined with Gaffer lamps, tempted to rip a page from *Jane Eyre* to make a quick telescope. She searched for buggies, searched for a man in an indigo coat, but he did not come.

"I am *angry with you."*

Ceony pressed her forehead to the glass. "I'm sorry," she whispered. She didn't know how else to get the message through. *I was stupid, I didn't think. I'm sorry that I endangered Delilah and Magician Hughes and you. Please believe me. If I could go back in time and stop myself, I would. I love you.*

She touched her cheek, prodding the healing bruise there. She had deserved that much.

She waited at the window for a long time, watching the people pass by, holding her breath whenever a rented buggy came down the street.

But Emery still didn't come.

CHAPTER 18

AFTER READING FIFTY PAGES of *Jane Eyre*, washing her clothes, and showing Langston the proper way to make gravy, Ceony bathed and managed to get into bed at a decent hour. While she didn't sleep well, she slept better than she had the night before, and found some relief in being able to wear a full-length skirt in the morning.

She searched for her little white bird at the window, but it hadn't returned. She hoped it had reached its destination safely, but if it had, that meant her family still lingered in the Mill Squats. Or someone did. Her imagination could only fathom who.

Her stomach turned sour, and she massaged it through her blouse. Langston had a telephone, didn't he? Perhaps she could ring Mg. Aviosky and learn something. Anything. She would fall like a soufflé otherwise.

As Ceony came down the stairs, she heard Langston speaking to someone in his living room. It only took a few steps for her to recognize the voice, and she nearly tripped the rest of the way to the main floor. Her heart once more lodged in her throat.

She hurried into the front room. "Emery . . . I mean, Magician Thane."

Emery stood by the front door, absent his indigo coat, or any coat for that matter. He wore only a white button-up shirt with long sleeves and a pair of dark-gray slacks. Had he donned a tie, he would have looked ready to work in an office. His face was newly shaved, and he'd cut his hair as well. It didn't look too different, just shorter and less unkempt.

He stood with his arms loosely folded across his ribs, leaning his weight on his left side. He glanced at her, the fire gone from his eyes.

He was beautiful.

Langston stood with him, fully dressed for the day, a pair of suspenders strapped over his shoulders. Ceony hadn't thought to try and overhear what they had been discussing, and she chided herself for it. Judging by their expressions, she assumed the conversation had involved her.

Ceony clasped her hands behind her back and fought down a flush. "I . . . didn't expect to see you so soon." *Only hoped.*

"We have a few things to discuss," Emery said. He didn't sound angry, just resigned. Resigned to what, Ceony couldn't tell, for Emery had shuttered his expression again, and she couldn't read the secrets behind his eyes. Curse whoever had taught him to do that.

Langston said, "Do you have anything to collect?"

"Just my shoes," Ceony said. Uneasy, she added, "I'll fetch them."

She hurried upstairs and retrieved the oxford shoes she had worn yesterday, taking a moment to inhale a few deep breaths and shake out her shoulders. Then she pinched her cheeks and hurried back downstairs.

Emery opened the door. "Thank you again, Langston. Let me know if you need that reference."

Langston nodded, then moved to tip his hat to Ceony, only to realize he wasn't wearing one. He settled for a nod and said, "Good day, and take care."

Ceony thanked him and stepped into the hallway. Emery guided her to the door with a hand on the small of her back. His other hand dug into his pocket and pulled out a Folded crane, its right wing crumpled from its confinement. Ceony's crane.

"These are not good ideas," he said.

Her gut sunk. So *he* had been at the house. "My family?"

"They're safe. Out of London."

"Thank you."

He nodded.

She took a deep breath. "So you met my parents."

"I did."

She wrung a handful of her skirt in her hands. "I really am sorry, Emery."

"I know," he said, quiet. "What's done is done, and in the end it didn't change much."

"Didn't change what, exactly?" she asked, but Emery didn't answer. He guided her out of the town house and into a buggy that already had its engine running, waiting for them.

Ceony noticed the suitcase sitting behind the seats. "Did you go back home?"

"Briefly."

After they had situated themselves and the buggy began to move, Emery asked, "Is there anything else I need to know, anything you've neglected to tell me?"

Ceony shook her head. "No. Except I lost your glider. That's how I got to the barn."

"Hmm," he replied, nodding. "I hope you closed the roof."

She hadn't.

They sat in silence, Ceony wringing her skirt until one of its buttons threatened to pop off. Emery noticed, for he placed a hand over hers to still the destruction.

"I'm not one to dump my autobiography on others," he said, his gaze on her hands, "but I've lost a number of things in my life—important things—and I have no desire to add you to that list, Ceony. Despite what you may think, I do care about you. My stewardship as your mentor aside, I've made your well-being my personal priority."

Ceony's pulse quickened at those words. Her chest felt hot.

Emery rested back against the buggy's seat. "Your family is safe, as promised. They'll be looked after until everything is settled."

"Thank you," she whispered.

"You're going to stay with Magician Aviosky for a while; she's agreed to the arrangement and will ensure your safety," he added. "I'm sure Delilah will appreciate the company."

Ceony had been about to ask after Delilah, but she reprocessed and said, "Why will I be staying with Magician Aviosky? Where will you be?"

She glanced back at the suitcase, then out the window, scanning the shops they passed: Briggs' Pharmacy, Wolf's Pencils. This wasn't the way to Mg. Aviosky's home. She watched the buildings and street signs glide past them, illuminated by the morning sun, and felt her whole body sink. "You're leaving. We're going to the train station."

"Very astute," Emery said.

She turned to him in her seat. "Where are you going? What are you going to do?"

He didn't look at her. "The same thing I've done for years."

"You're going after Grath," she hissed, keeping her voice low to prevent the driver from overhearing. "You're going after him yourself, and after you scolded me about it!"

He turned toward her, his face hovering very close to her own. "This is different, Ceony. I have experience. It's a decision that was made on behalf of Criminal Affairs. And I'm not going after Grath."

Ceony's anger stripped away in jagged pieces, replaced with quivering fear. "Saraj," she whispered. "You're going after Saraj."

He frowned, but nodded.

The buggy pulled up beside the train station just as a clock stand on the sidewalk chimed the eighth hour.

Ceony grabbed Emery's arm to keep him from leaving. "No, Emery!" she pleaded, blinking back tears. "How do you even know where he is? Where will you go? How long will you be away?"

"I either don't know or can't tell you," he said. He looked . . . guilty.

Ceony opened her mouth to reply, but then addressed the driver instead. "Could you step out of the auto for just a moment, please?"

The driver nodded and stepped outside, looking pleased enough with the arrangement. He pulled a fag and match from his pocket.

"I went through a lot of grief trying to keep you alive," Ceony said, "and now you're going to get yourself killed!"

Emery actually smiled. "You have so little faith in me."

"You're going after a man who can kill with a swipe of his hand!" Ceony cried. "Please reconsider. I'll do anything. I'll never leave the cottage again. You can transfer me, if you want. I'll give you my stipend. Just please, *please* don't go."

Emery's expression softened. Lifting his hand, he gently touched the bruise on Ceony's cheek, a caress that sent chills running down her jaw and neck. "I know more about how to deal with these men than most, Ceony," he said. "And this way, I can personally guarantee your safety. Please, trust me on this. This time, you can't change my mind."

He tucked a stray lock of hair behind Ceony's ear, then pulled back and retrieved his suitcase from behind the buggy's seat. Ceony watched him, numb and wordless. Her heart slowed in her chest. Her fingers trembled.

Emery opened the buggy door and stepped out into the sunlight.

He was going to face Saraj Prendi, on his own.

This might be the last time Ceony ever saw him.

"I do care about you."

She stared out the glassless window as he walked toward the station, suitcase in hand, the sun spinning gold into his raven hair.

Her pulse quickened until her skin throbbed with her heartbeat. Ceony scrambled across the seat and grabbed the door latch, kicking the door open. She jumped outside, blinking the bright morning from her eyes.

Then she shouted, "If you're going to get yourself killed, you could at least kiss me first!"

Emery paused, as did two other men heading for the train. He turned around and looked to her, the sun pouring around him like a halo.

He walked back to the buggy, and Ceony flushed. Had she upset him? Was he really going to . . . ?

Emery set down his luggage. He put one hand on Ceony's waist, the other on the unbruised side of her face, and pulled her away from the buggy.

Turning his head carefully to the right, he bent down and kissed her.

His warm lips pressed into hers, and Ceony's entire body seemed to turn inside out. The sun's bright rays pierced through her. The city fell away piece by piece.

She closed her eyes and reached for Emery's neck, kissing him as she'd always wanted to kiss him, parting her lips against his, savoring him, relishing him.

The kiss lasted an eternity, and yet only a few moments. Emery pulled away slowly, leaving Ceony aching for him. She stared up into the beauty of his green eyes, and for a moment she saw everything there, all the pieces of his heart that she remembered so vividly, all the smiles and unspoken words she had earned since meeting him three months earlier.

Emery again touched his lips to her forehead, then stepped back and picked up his suitcase. He didn't say anything more, and Ceony didn't speak as he set off for the train. There was nothing left to say. Nothing that hadn't already been said, in one way or another.

Ceony watched the paper magician leave, her hands clutched over her hard-beating heart. Then he vanished, and Ceony had no choice but to slide back into the buggy and offer direction to Mg. Aviosky's home, as well as a silent prayer that Emery would return to her unscathed.

CHAPTER 19

CEONY THANKED THE DRIVER when she disembarked at Mg. Aviosky's home—a tall, gothic structure that rested on its own corner of the street, where the main city eased into a suburb. Charcoal-colored shingles covered both its gabled roof and a turret, behind which rested a narrow chimney free of smoke. It boasted a long porch behind a short, spindled fence, and the decorative columns holding up the second story looked as if they had been stolen from giant sitting-room chairs. Ceony had been to the house thrice before, once for the celebration for her graduation from the Tagis Praff School for the Magically Inclined—before Mg. Aviosky announced that Ceony had been assigned to Folding; once to visit Delilah; and once two days ago, when Mg. Aviosky had pulled her from that awful basement in Belgium.

Yet as Ceony trudged up the steps to the house—somewhat surprised that Mg. Aviosky hadn't come outside to meet her—her heart and mind lingered at the train station. Emery had likely boarded his train by now. If only she could have followed him and found out its destination. Surely not far, unless Saraj had left town.

And if the deadly Excisioner *had* left town, Ceony wished the Magicians' Cabinet would leave it at that and let Emery stay.

She rubbed two fingers against her chest as she rang the bell, trying to soothe the pain between her lungs. She imagined a canyon much like the one she had seen in Emery's heart forming there. If he didn't make it back to her, she knew it would rip her in two. Criminal Affairs had protected her family, but why couldn't they also have protected the man she loved?

She licked her lips and allowed herself a moment of gratitude for her good memory. Whatever happened, she would always remember *that*, down to the very last, minute detail. As she closed her eyes and relished the memory, her knees turned weak. *Oh, Emery, please don't get yourself killed.*

No one answered the door, so Ceony knocked. She wondered if she'd be able to retrieve her things from the flat, but surely two Gaffers could manage to collect her belongings for her. And her stay would be temporary. Only a week, surely. Maybe two.

Stepping back from the door, Ceony peered in the direction of the train station, straining to hear one of its whistles over the sounds of the city. She heard nothing but silence and the melody of an unseen songbird in the crabapple tree shading the left half of Mg. Aviosky's yard.

She sighed and tested the knob. Finding it unlocked, she let herself in.

The house opened onto stairs leading to the second floor and a hallway leading deeper into the first. Ceony peered into the front room lit with streaks of sunlight that pushed through the closed blinds.

"Magician Aviosky?" Ceony called. "Delilah?"

Odd that they weren't home. Given the circumstances, Mg. Aviosky should have been awaiting Ceony's arrival. She was too rigid not to be.

Her stomach suddenly felt drained. She slapped the back of her neck, thinking she felt a bug crawling over her skin, but it was only a wisp of hair.

Slipping off her shoes—Mg. Aviosky had particular rules concerning shoes on her carpet—Ceony pulled herself up the eleven stairs to the second floor, which held the library, the living room, and a long hallway filled with mirrors and bedroom doors. Delilah's room was the third on the right, but Ceony found it empty, as was the bathroom and what she assumed to be Mg. Aviosky's room, judging by the size and lack of décor.

She heard shuffling from the third floor. They had to be in the study or the mirror room, then. Perhaps Delilah was in the middle of a lesson.

Ceony wound around to the last set of stairs and climbed them, the boards creaking under her feet. Unlike in Emery's cottage, the third floor of Mg. Aviosky's home was the smallest, and it bore only three rooms—the large mirror room where Delilah practiced her craft, Mg. Aviosky's study, and a tiny room for storage.

"Magician Aviosky?" Ceony called. She reached for the door to the mirror room, but it swung open before she could touch the knob. The man on the other side filled the entire doorway, and his sharp canines gleamed with a light all their own.

"Hello, pet." Grath grinned.

Ceony sucked in air for a scream and stumbled backward, but Grath's meaty hand shot out and grabbed her by the valley between her neck and shoulder, digging his nails into the muscle there. He yanked Ceony into the mirror room, which was bathed in sunlight from the uncovered windows. Misty clouds had begun to crawl across the sky.

Ceony's feet lost the floor as Grath hefted her eye-level with him. Grinning wider, he shifted his weight and threw her onto the floorboards. The wood thudded under her kneecaps, and her joints screamed in retaliation. The skin over her left knee broke, and Ceony finally managed to get air over her vocal cords. The result sounded like a mix between a gasp and a whimper.

Shaking herself, Ceony pushed her body up. The first thing she saw was her own reflection in an antique mirror on the wall beside her. Two large, multipaned windows hovered over her, and the space between them was crowded with more mirrors and tables filled with blown glass, glass beads, and glass shards. Then she saw Delilah's reflection in a tall mirror made of Gaffer's glass—the same mirror she had stumbled out of on her return from Belgium.

Ceony scrambled to her feet. Delilah had been tied to a chair with coarse rope, her white handkerchief knotted and stuffed into her mouth. She tried to cry out, but the gag muted her words. Tears spilled from her wide, brown eyes.

Beside her stood—no, hung—Mg. Aviosky, her toes barely touching the ground, her arms stretched up over her head and tied with more rope, which had been slung over a hook in the ceiling, meant to hold a chandelier. Mg. Aviosky's head lolled to one side, and her glasses sat crooked on her nose, the right lens cracked.

She was unconscious, and her hands had turned a ghostly white, her forearms purple.

"No!" Ceony shouted, running for the magicians, but Grath found her hair and yanked her back, pulling several orange strands from her scalp in the process. Ceony's back collided with Grath's wide chest, and he wrapped a thick arm around her neck.

"I'd hoped you would come, Ceony," he said into her ear, low and snakelike. Delilah squirmed in her chair, screaming futilely against her gag. "I thought you should be the first to know that I figured out our little secret. Chasing you all over Europe gave me time to think about it, as did our chats about Lira."

"Let them go!" Ceony pleaded. She dug her nails into Grath's arm, but it didn't seem to faze him. She kicked her legs, but couldn't find a good angle to strike him. "Please, do whatever you want with me, but let them go. They're not part of this!"

"Oh, but they are," Grath said. He released Ceony and spun her around, then shoved her against the wall. A small, triangular mirror toppled onto the floor, cracking into thirds. Sharp pain radiated in her shoulder blades.

"They're all part of this," he continued. "I'll make them part of this, and I'll let you watch. Let you know how it feels to be able to do *nothing* while your loved ones die."

"She's not dead!" Ceony protested. "Lira, she's just frozen—"

"I'll take care of Lira," Grath spat. He reached out and dug his knuckle into the bruise on Ceony's cheek, making her cry out. "I'll take care of her. I know it all; I just need the power first. But this time, I won't let you get in the way."

He pulled her off the wall, one hand under her armpit and the other around her neck, and slammed her into the window. Ceony struggled against the fingers pressing into her windpipe.

With the slightest smirk pulling at the corner of his mouth, Grath said, "Shatter."

The window shattered, and Ceony choked on a scream as the fragments of glass pushed their way into her skin, past her shirt and chemise, tearing her skirt and stockings. Glass embedded itself up and down her back and into her neck. It flew past her shoulders, slicing open fabric and skin. It stabbed like hundreds of tiny daggers into the back of her legs and knees. Fiery darts of pain pricked her body and dozens of small rivers of blood drizzled over her skin.

She gasped, a fish out of water, and Grath released her, letting her drop like a broken doll onto the floor. Bits of glass small as an infant's fingernails were embedded in the skin of her hand, and star-shaped crisscrosses adorned her arms. Blood soaked her sleeves, and from what she could see in the mirrors, it soaked her back as well.

The blood may as well have been acid given the way her skin burned around the glass.

She tried to move, tried to push herself up, but the angry shards dug deeper into her skin, searing like hot coals. She wheezed and let herself go limp on the floor, cutting the side of her face on yet more broken gems of glass.

Grath brushed off his hands and grinned. "You see, Ceony," he said, pacing the room back toward Delilah and Aviosky, "it *is* about the words, and it *is* about the material." He patted Delilah on the cheek; she had gone still in her binds. "I kept thinking of Lira, my dear Lira, and how to cure this obnoxious hex you placed on her. I knew I had to reverse it. And I thought, *Reverse*. Yes, that makes sense, doesn't it? Reverse the spell.

"Binding is a spell, too, you know," he continued, tapping one hand against the other behind his back. "But all spells have counters, a 'Cease' command or the like. So why shouldn't the Binding spell have one, too?"

Ceony held her breath and tried to move, groaning against the sensation of the glass shards shifting in her skin. Her hand slipped in blood, and she collapsed back onto the floorboards.

Grath smirked and paced, this time closer to her. "So I studied, I tested, I practiced like a good apprentice. But I was still missing something. I had to step outside the frame, so to speak, and really analyze what I wanted to achieve. And last night I figured it out while I was staring into the very mirror you left me at that restaurant. Do you want to know what I learned?"

Ceony's fingers slid across the floor, catching on a bloodied pyramid of glass.

"Me!" Grath announced, lifting his hands in a grand gesture. "The missing piece is me. Clever, isn't it?"

"Deli . . . lah," Ceony groaned, trying to slide across the floorboards. She felt hot liquid bubble up from her back and winced.

"Don't you see?" Grath asked, strolling back toward Delilah and Mg. Aviosky. "I *am* the key! I must rebond to *myself*."

Ceony blinked, his words taking a moment to register. "P-Please . . ."

Grath talked over her. "Let me show you, explain it real slow. First, you must have the raw original, as I like to call it."

He pulled a small satchel off his belt and dumped its contents onto the table. Fine, tan sand poured over the surface. Blower's sand, used for forming glass. The raw original . . . The natural elements castable materials were made of?

"Second," he continued, "is to reverse the process, the words. Do you remember what the words are?"

Hair fell into Ceony's eyes.

"Come now," Grath said, sliding a glass dagger from his belt. He held it to Delilah's collar, and she whimpered beneath her gag as he lightly drew the blade across her skin. "Tell me the words."

Ceony began to tremble, a motion that felt entirely involuntary.

"M-Material . . . made by man," Ceony whispered, "I summon you. L-Link t-to me . . ."

"Yes, that's it," Grath interrupted, cutting her short. He stuck his right hand into the sand and said, "This is the tricky part. Material made by *earth*, your handler summons you. Unlink to me as I link through you, unto this very day."

Warm blood streaked over the side of Ceony's neck. She could feel her pulse radiating in every single cut and gouge, could hear it drumming Delilah's name in her ears.

"Next, bond to myself," Grath continued. He pressed the same hand into his chest and said, "Material made by man, I summon you. Link to me as I link to you, unto this very day."

He pulled his hand back and crouched, ensuring Ceony could meet his gaze.

"And then," he said, low and slow, "you bond to the *new* material. I promised I'd show you, didn't I?"

He stood and shoved Delilah's chair against the wall, then wrapped his fingers around her neck.

"No!" Ceony cried, pushing against the floor. Her knees slid in blood, and electric pain soared up her legs and into her shoulder blades, stealing her breath away.

"Are you watching?" Grath asked, his eyes locked on to Delilah. "Material made by man, your creator summons you.

"Do you know how an Excisioner bonds, Ceony?"

"Grath, no!" Ceony cried, pushing herself up. Her arms turned to fire. New rivers of blood burst from the skin on her back, ringing around her ribs and torso.

"Link to me as I link to you through my years, until the day I die—"

Ceony grabbed the antique mirror and pulled herself to her feet.

"And become earth," Grath finished.

A choking sound emanated from Delilah's throat. Her eyes widened, and blood began to pour from her nostrils. She stared at Grath, fright emanating from her gaze, until her eyes rolled back into her head.

Grath released her, and she went limp in the chair.

"No!" Ceony screamed, running for her. "Delilah, no! No!"

Grath swung his arm out, colliding with Ceony's chest. She fell backward, shoving the shards of glass in her back even deeper into her skin. She cried out and sputtered, tasting iron on her lips. Shadows bordered her vision.

"Oh, I'm not done yet," Grath said, flexing and unflexing his hand. He smiled and turned to Mg. Aviosky.

Ceony's body pulsed with pain. She struggled to stand as Grath neared Mg. Aviosky, but her limbs went limp. Too much. Never had she been so torn and tattered; never had she *hurt* like this, inside and out.

She stared at Delilah, who looked little more than a paper doll.

She looked at the shards of glass surrounding her, speckling the floorboards like misshapen diamonds.

Speckling the floorboards.

The *wooden* floorboards.

Ceony had no paper, but she had this.

Pressing her bloodied palm to the floor, she murmured, barely audible even to her own ears, "Material made by earth, your handler summons you. Unlink to me as I link through you, unto this very day."

She pressed the same hand to herself and whimpered, "Material made by man, I summon you. Link to me as I link to you, unto this very day."

She pushed herself up on her elbow, her spirit somewhere distant, far away from the hot, searing pain of her injuries. She reached for a large shard of glass and clutched it in her hands, its edges cutting into her fingers.

Grath stopped before Aviosky and pulled apart her blouse, then used his knife to slice through her camisole, revealing her chest. Her heart.

"Material made by man," Ceony said, almost more in her head than out loud, "your creator summons you. Link to me as I link to you through my years, until the day I die and become earth."

The glass tingled in her fingers. Delilah's glass. It had worked.

Grath pulled back his hand.

Ceony's eyes darted between the mirrors. She saw her bloodied shoulder in a round one just beside Grath's head, reflected from the antique mirror against the wall.

She remembered Delilah sitting across from her at the bistro, bubbly and alive, *so alive*, laughing at the prank she had pulled with the makeup compact. Remembered her explanation of the spell.

Turning to the antique mirror, which she had already touched, Ceony whispered "Reflect" and concentrated on Lira as she had first seen her, a beauty in Emery's kitchen, black clothes hugging her perfect curves, the twisted ruby smile on her lips. She imagined Lira's chocolate-colored curls and the way they'd framed her face and spilled over her shoulders. She remembered the dark glint to her eyes, the vials of blood hanging off her belt.

Sure enough, the antique mirror produced a perfect reflection of Lira, and the round mirror picked up the image of her face in turn.

Grath noticed. He hesitated, spying Lira's reflection in the corner of his eye. He spun, perhaps expecting her to be standing right behind him. Perhaps expecting her to be cured.

Turning his back to Ceony.

Ceony pushed off the ground, growling through the pain. She collided into Grath and dug the shard of glass in her hand into his back, right below his rib cage.

"Shatter!" she cried.

The glass shattered in her hands, breaking into dozens of pieces beneath Grath's skin.

Grath choked. He grabbed Ceony by the hair and threw her off him; she collided with the floor again and shrieked as spilled glass mangled her already bloodied arm.

Grath stumbled into Mg. Aviosky, grabbing at her for support, but his legs gave out from under him. He collapsed at Delilah's feet. The glass in his body had cut him too deep, too quickly. He hadn't prepared a Healing spell beforehand.

The shadows lacing Ceony's vision expanded, sucking color from the room. Her own blood looked gray, as if melting clouds had smeared over her skin.

She crawled to the nearest mirror, which sat just beside the table covered in sand. Grunting, she touched her fingers to it, leaving prints of red against her reflection.

Help. She needed help . . . Her foggy mind pulled up the memory of the spell Delilah had used on the broken mirror in Ceony's flat, and with a voice more air than sound, she said, "Reverse."

Her reflection vanished, replaced by a bright room filled with white furniture and ornate vases. A gray cat sat on a sofa, licking one of its paws. A polished banister marked a staircase in the back. Someone's sitting room.

The shadows filled Ceony's vision, and she dropped her hand and head to the floor. She could have sworn she heard Mg. Hughes calling out her name.

CHAPTER 20

Emery

LONDON RUSHED BY EMERY'S window, the blocks and points of city architecture shrinking as the main city dwindled down into its residential branches. Flats gradually morphed into homes, which grew farther and farther apart as the train chugged its way south. Emery watched rolling farms, brush, and sparse trees, pass by in smears of green, stared at waterways so still they looked like Gaffer's glass. He moved farther from home and closer to his enemy, yet he couldn't comprehend the rush of colors and the drag of distance around him. In the back of his mind his thoughts pieced together illusions, chains, and careful Folds. In the front, it thought, *Ceony.*

How long had it been since he'd last kissed a woman? His mind calculated the math sluggishly. Three years? After the separation, before the divorce. Memories he would prefer not to entertain.

Emery leaned his elbow on the window of the train car. Ceony. One month ago he had played with the idea of courting her once she'd earned her magicianship and they'd both settled into their new lives, she as a budding Folder and he with the next sorry lout Patrice forced his way. He had no doubt that Ceony would pass her Folding tests at the end of the minimum two years' apprenticeship. She had proved herself bright and eager to learn, and her remarkable memory still astounded him.

Yet in recent weeks that amount of time—two years—had begun to seem longer and longer. The squares of his calendar grew bigger, and the hands on clocks moved slower. Revealing so much of himself to one person, even if not by choice, had changed something between them. Created in a matter of days a deep, comfortable bond that often took years to achieve. Her cheer, her dedication, and her beauty made that bond that much harder to ignore, no matter how hard he tried to reason himself out of it.

And her food. Good heavens, everything that woman touched turned to gold in his mouth. She'd make him fatter than Langston before her year mark passed.

A smile touched his lips. He had grown accustomed to living on his own. The two years he'd spent alone in that cottage with just Jonto for company had never bothered him, save in retrospect. Perhaps it was some great fortune or—God forbid—an act of karma that had brought Ceony into his life to light up a house that he hadn't realized had gone dark. A light he wouldn't have been able to see if not for her utter stupidity in following an Excisioner clear to the coast for the sake of saving his life. She'd barely known him then. Now she knew everything.

Almost everything.

Emery refocused on the landscape flying by his window. Had he already passed Caterham? Perhaps time had finally decided to catch up to him. He only hoped it wouldn't move too fast when he needed it most.

A man in a brown suit sat in the far seat across from him. Emery ignored his presence.

Emery had only faced Saraj personally once in his life, shortly after Lira had thrown her soul to the wind and run off with Grath and whoever else the Excisioner—no, Gaffer—had enchanted at the time. The Saraj was vermin, twisted like taffy and more insane than the world's worst criminals. A man who would kill countless people for sport, who raped women and boasted about it to his pursuers. A man who stood outside society and fished into it with a jagged spear.

Grath was the only man Emery knew of who could befriend— and possibly control—Saraj, and if Hughes succeeded in capturing him, who knew what Saraj would do next, where he would go. The thought of him taking one more step toward Ceony drove Emery mad, made his fingertips itch and his stomach writhe. And so Emery had agreed to this last hurrah, this careful attempt to capture Saraj before he went wild. Emery wondered how much wilder the Excisioner could become.

He didn't plan to find out. The train headed toward what he hoped would be Saraj's last stand. Emery would see the man caged, and Emery would survive. He had to.

He finally had someone worth going home to.

———

The train arrived in Brighton near noon. Emery hired an automobile to Rottingdean, and then walked from there to Saltdean, on the coast.

Saltdean had once been known for smuggling, thanks to its high, salt-crusted cliffs and the hidden trenches that made unlicensed docking easy and discreet. Emery could taste the salt in the air, but not the sea. To him, it tasted too much like blood.

Off the coast and far into the English Channel, he saw a storm sweeping off France. He wondered if it would reach him today. He would need to be careful about where he laid his spells. Hughes had said the others wouldn't arrive until the next day.

Suitcase still in hand, Emery took a stroll around Saltdean, examining its cliffs. He headed into the town, eyeing its sparse buildings and scattered homes. He needed to find somewhere large, but uninhabited. Such parameters shouldn't be hard to come by in a town like this one. He wanted to stay away from the town's north end, where the common people had begun to turn the land into something profitable.

He found a medium-sized factory, three floors, still intact and in decent condition, albeit weathered from storms. It smelled like it had been a shoe factory, but most of its interior had already been gutted. It would do.

Emery started the trek back to Rottingdean. He had a great deal of paper to buy.

Emery slept little, thanks to a friendly version of insomnia that often let him choose when he did and did not suffer from it. He spent most of the night carefully Folding papers large and small, both for his personal use and in preparation for the showdown at the factory. His calloused fingers worked four-pointed stars, links for a shield chain and a snaring chain, and anything else his mind could conjure. As for the factory . . . he could only hope Juliet managed to keep up her end of the plan and had successfully driven Saraj to Saltdean. If she didn't, it would all be for naught.

In the morning Emery went to a back alley by a condemned tackle shop near the factory, the place he had designated as the rendezvous point. Two automobiles pulled in shortly after nine, carrying Mg. Cantrell and several police officers. Juliet, a Smelter, was roughly the same age as Emery and had joined Criminal Affairs two years ago after a successful—albeit short—career as a deputy inspector in Nottingham. A pretty woman and tall, she walked with a military-type stride and a chronic stiffness to her shoulders. Like Patrice, she wore her dark hair pulled into a tight bun, which emphasized her square jaw. Four policemen whose gait and posture implied a background in the military accompanied her.

"I'd say you're looking well, Emery," she said as she approached, hands clasped behind her back, "but I'm afraid you aren't. Poor sleep? Perhaps it's the lighting."

She glanced up at the overcast sky.

Emery didn't bother with small talk. He liked Juliet well enough, but it felt like a waste of breath. "Is he coming?"

"Everything seems to be on schedule," she said, walking up the road. The policemen followed in their auto at a crawling pace. "We'll need to set up quickly, be prepared. Saraj Prendi doesn't run a tight ship."

"I've made preparations. An old shoe factory, up this way." Emery gestured. From within his coat—the sage-green one—he pulled free a shield chain and offered it to her.

Juliet shook her head and held up a hand; the automobile stopped behind them. "Thank you, but it's unnecessary," she said, circling back to the trunk of the auto. Emery followed her. She opened a latch and, from a thick cardboard box, pulled free a steel-cast chain, the links forming a wide band. "Wear this," she said. "It won't crumble if it gets wet."

Emery didn't complain, merely nodded and took the new shield chain from the Smelter. It weighed far more than its paper cousin, but Juliet was right—it was much more durable. Folding had its limits in defensive spells. Offensive, as well. But every material had its strengths and weaknesses. Emery had internalized that truth during his own apprenticeship, which he had completed nine years ago.

"The others are stationed in Brighton," Juliet said, digging through a jacket pocket to find an address. "Send a bird to them, if you will. They're the only warning we'll get when Saraj arrives."

Emery accepted the address, and Juliet pulled a lightweight, gray cardstock from the back of the automobile, perfect for camouflaging against the dreary sky. Emery Folded it carefully, forming a sturdy songbird with instructions to return upon its release, just as a true bird would.

"Juliet."

"Hmm?"

Emery weighed the songbird in his palm. "Did they find the shed? Lira?"

The Smelter frowned. "Alfred says the local police found the sheds, even the broken mirror, but not her. Not yet."

The words bothered him, but not the way he'd expected. He didn't feel that familiar jab in his chest or the drip of anxiety. He felt a horsefly biting at him. He brushed it off—Lira was the least of his worries right now.

"Breathe," Emery murmured to the songbird, and the small creature awoke in his hands. He whispered its mission, and the bird flew up from his hands, catching the wind westward toward Brighton.

Juliet sighed. "I hope it doesn't rain."

"It won't," Emery said. "Not yet."

She scoffed. "Can you be so sure?"

"Folders always are," he replied, turning from the auto. "Let me show you the factory. Then we'll station your men."

———

Time sped forward the moment the paper bird returned.

Attuned to Emery, it found him where he hid behind the tackle shop with Juliet, flapping its now crinkled wings to land in his palm. It looked weathered and a little beaten, but still functional.

"Cease," Emery said, and he turned the bird over. A short message was written in tiny inked words on the underside of the right wing: *Staged chase, heading toward Saltdean. S may be low on blood. Cannot teleport.*

Saraj Prendi was headed straight for them.

Emery passed the bird to Juliet, who pressed her lips into a thin line. "If the boys don't get him here, my mines will. I've blocked any escape to the coast and farther inland, and they're rigged only to blow when they sense his blood. After that . . . I hope your tricks are foolproof, Emery Thane."

"If not," he replied, "then I am a fool."

It didn't take long for Saraj to announce himself—a paper bird could only travel so much faster than a man. Gunshots echoed through the still, stale air of Saltdean. Not Saraj's guns, but those belonging to the men who chased him. Perhaps they were trying to make killing shots, or the blasts could be a warning.

An explosion followed, close enough that Emery could hear sediment bouncing off the tackle shop—one of Juliet's mines, forcing Saraj toward the factory and away from the coast.

Juliet actually smiled, her eyes narrowing. "See you there," she said. She leapt out from behind the tackle shop, pulling from her jacket several farthing-sized bronze discs, which she threw out with the command, "Target!" The discs spun wildly in midair and shot forward, buzzing with the movement. Juliet ran after them.

Emery counted to eight before running the opposite way, looping around a hill toward the factory. A gust of wind pushed hair into his eyes, and then the breeze filled with dark, red smoke just before it died.

Emery staggered to a stop, his shoes skidding against the incline. Not ten feet before him stood Saraj Prendi, grinning with too-white teeth. So he *did* have enough blood to teleport.

Saraj was a lithe man in his late thirties, though perhaps he was older, for his dark skin hid what Emery normally used as signs of aging. He stood three inches taller than Emery, with narrow shoulders and long, thin arms. His narrow head came to a sharp point at the chin, and thick curls of hair stuck out unfashionably above either ear. Gold studs shimmered in his earlobes despite the lack of sun. He wore a workman's clothes in the English style, girded about with leathers. Like Lira, he had a belt equipped with vials of cold blood, several of them empty. Only the heavens knew who had perished to fill his stock.

"Emery Thane," he said in a smooth voice, higher than what one might have expected. "The peak of health, and yet still I move faster. Curious. I'd hoped we would run into each other, you and I. You are always the wall between me and my favorite quarries."

Emery offered a mock bow, careful to keep his eyes on the Excisioner. "I'll offer the first dance, but I want to know something. Why the paper mill? Why any of this? Grath wanted Ceony alive, so what's your ploy?"

Saraj grinned. "It's a dull game, *kagaz*," he said, using the Hindi word for paper. "Grath has been a real—what's the word? Dog. *Mongrel*, ever since your old pet went cold. Sniffing at doors for bones. I wanted to move on, but I couldn't do that with Little Red anchoring Grath in England, hmm?"

Emery's hand flew to his right coat pocket and grabbed a fistful of Folded throwing stars, which he threw toward Saraj in a wide spray. The Excisioner dodged, but not before a gunshot echoed between them and a wide gash opened on Saraj's bare shoulder.

Shadows danced in Saraj's dark eyes as Juliet and another policeman charged up the hill toward them, the latter reloading his gun. Grinning at Emery, Saraj pranced backward and ran for cover in the factory, breaking through an already cracked window to do so.

"Do *not* let him leave," Juliet said breathlessly to her uniformed companion. "Station yourself and Smith at the back exits." Then she shouted, "The rest with me!"

Emery's pulse raced, filling him with a sick sort of energy that had him sprinting after Juliet, his coat fanning out like a cape behind him. The chain around his torso clinked like narrow bells, offering him some reassurance. Still, now more than ever, he needed his guard up.

He went through the front door after the others and made sure to lock it. Saraj wouldn't leave this building alive, save for in chains. He hated to think of what would happen if England lost yet another Folder. He really should start charging for these things.

Saraj hadn't gone far; he stood at the opposite end of a large, open room with a high ceiling and stained windows, a few of them chipped or broken. A handful of bent gears and shredded cables littered the floor, left behind when the factory had been gutted. Old barrels lined the walls alongside empty crates. Other than the door behind Emery, there were two exits in the room, both near Saraj. One led into a long hallway that ended in a set of stairs; the other opened into another, smaller room with two doors. Juliet had soldered shut the right-hand door that led outside. The second door opened onto a hallway leading to storage and supply rooms.

If Saraj chose the first door, the left door, he would be ultimately cornering himself. If he chose the right . . . Emery prayed he would choose the right.

But he didn't run. He stood in a wide-legged stance, rolling a vial of blood back and forth in his already crimson-stained hand. His other hand hovered near a golden pistol at his hip.

Juliet moved first, waving her hand and shouting, "Attract!"

The chain around Emery's torso shifted as though drawn to Juliet, but the spell hadn't been aimed at him. Saraj's pistol leapt from its holster as though magnetized—it *had* been magnetized— and flew from his reach before he could snatch it back, sailing between the three policemen who'd entered the room with Juliet and snapping into place on a metallic belt around the Smelter's hips.

Another clamor of metal on metal drew Emery's eyes to a small knife that had also made the journey to her belt. Emery hadn't even seen the blade leave Saraj's person.

Unfortunately, the vials of blood—the Excisioner's strongest ammo—were made of glass.

Juliet pulled her own gun: a sleek revolver with an ivory handle that would make Ceony croon with jealousy. "All our firearms are enchanted, Prendi," she said, louder than necessary. Her voice carried authority. "They won't miss their targets. Surrender now."

Saraj only smiled. Emery didn't see him uncork the vial, but he flung out his hand, using the same aerial push Lira had favored in combat.

Juliet's chain tightened around her torso. A free strand of hair from her bun fluttered as though caught in the wind, but the rest of her remained unscathed.

"How clever," Saraj said, his words lightly accented. "I had hoped you'd offer a challenge."

"Fire!" Juliet shouted.

Saraj darted to the right, but not toward the exit. Gunfire thundered through the large room. Splashes of blood flew from Saraj's vials, leaving small puddles on the floor that rose up like rooted ghosts. The bullets changed course for them, missing Saraj.

He used his *own* blood, then. The enchanted bullets couldn't detect the difference. Clever.

Saraj rounded the room as policemen fired, heading toward Emery—dangerously close to the window through which he had entered. Emery darted forward to meet him, pulling a flash star from his coat—paper Folded to look like the head of an intricate pinwheel. He tossed it forward and shouted, "Flash!"

Bright, white light pulsed out of the star's center, so blinding that even Emery, its caster, saw dark spots before his eyes. Saraj stumbled, blinking rapidly.

He regained his balance quickly and lunged toward Emery, making Emery's shield chain clamp around his chest. Then Saraj moved again, but this time he rolled to the side and shoved two of the barrels lining the room, one with each hand. The first collided with Juliet. The second slammed into Emery like an automobile at full speed.

The impact knocked the air from his lungs and sent sharp pain coursing through his ribs. Emery's feet left the floor and he sailed backward until he collided with the factory wall, shoulder first.

He heard a *snap* and hit the floor. The pain exploded soon after.

His lungs found air and he gasped as hot agony coursed through his collar, up the right side of his neck, and down his right arm, pulsing and unrelenting, twisting like a drill. He rolled onto his left shoulder to relieve some of the pressure. His collarbone jutted at a sad angle, but it hadn't broken the skin. A relief—leaving a mess of his blood for Saraj was as good as letting the Excisioner touch his skin.

He shook his head and pushed himself upright with his left arm, grinding his teeth as the break shifted. Juliet picked herself up off the floor, too. The policemen had been busy while they were incapacitated, thankfully. Two of them had outmaneuvered Saraj's blood clones and landed their bullets, and blood flowed steadily from Saraj's right hip and right pectoral. The Excisioner had covered the latter wound with one hand and was quietly chanting. When he dropped his arm, the hole had vanished. A Healing spell, and well timed.

Before the others could reload their pistols, Saraj lashed out at the nearest policeman and grabbed him by the throat, turning him about to use him as a shield.

No, Emery had been mistaken. Saraj snapped the man's neck while the others looked on, helpless, and let him drop to the floor in a heap.

Saraj charged for Juliet, pulling from his pocket not a vial of blood, but of teeth.

Lifting himself onto his knees, Emery pulled free his snaring chain from his frock and swept it outward with the command, "Snare!" The tip of the chain snagged Saraj's ankle just before he met—*touched*—the Smelter. The enchanted yellow teeth flew by Juliet and embedded themselves in the opposite wall like tiny bullets.

Emery leapt to his feet—a knifelike pain blazing through his collar—and jerked back his arm. Saraj fell onto one knee, but kicked his leg hard enough to tear the chain. The spell fell to the ground, lifeless.

Saraj danced backward as Juliet finished reloading her gun. He pushed another barrel into one of the two remaining police officers. The man collapsed against the far wall, unmoving.

Emery reached for his Burst spell as Saraj, chanting, returned to the man with the broken neck and plunged his hand into his chest, pulling out his heart.

Emery ran forward and shouted, "Don't let him use it!"

Juliet switched her aim and fired, piercing the center of the heart with her bullet, ruining it. Saraj cursed and dropped it. The bullet had embedded into his palm, mixing the Excisioner's blood with that of the fallen policeman.

Saraj's good hand ran over the lips of his vials, counting corks. He was running low on ammunition—they all knew it—but with Juliet's finger on the trigger, he had no time to collect from the policeman's body. Saraj laughed, a high-pitched, maniacal sound. He uttered a few words, and the blood within the dead man's body began to boil, filling the room with acrid steam. Saraj darted backward, taking the right exit just as Juliet fired her gun. Her bullet embedded into the wall, just missing the Excisioner. The bullets had been enchanted to hit their targets, but they couldn't bend around corners.

The last policeman ran after Saraj, both hands on his gun, and Juliet followed at his heels. Holding up his right arm with his left, Emery chased after them, urging his body to fly, biting his tongue against the searing grinding in his collarbone. His eyes burned as he passed through the red steam, holding his breath.

Emery scrambled through the smaller room with the outside-leading door, noting a bloodied handprint on the wall. At the end of the hallway he caught up with Juliet, who was chasing Saraj into the storage rooms.

Red spotted the long sheet of paper lying on the floor and shoes had crinkled it, but it would still work. Emery ran over to it, then beckoned it upward with a single command: "Connect."

Juliet and the policeman both leveled their guns at Saraj, who was still cackling, a blood vial in his hand.

"You should know no wall can hold me," he said with glee. "Next time we'll play on my board, yes?"

He threw down the vial, its cold contents splattering over the floor. It took only a second for Saraj's face to fall. He had tried to teleport, but the blood didn't heed him.

Wide-eyed, he lunged for a window and punched it, only to withdraw bloody knuckles. The window wasn't made of glass. It didn't exist, save as an illusion. Saraj's fist had collided with the cement wall of the room—the wall behind the paper illusion masking the inside of the giant blind box that Emery had just sealed behind them.

Saraj's magic wouldn't work in here, but the firearms would.

"Hands up before I blow them off," Juliet spat.

Saraj grinned. The sound of the revolver firing startled Emery; Juliet had shot Saraj in the calf.

The Excisioner raised his hands and dropped to his knees, seemingly unfazed by pain. "Well played," he wheezed. He started chanting as the policeman came forward with cuffs. No, not chanting, singing. Emery picked out the lyrics.

In and out the Eagle
That's the way the money goes
Pop! Goes the weasel . . .

Emery crouched, not wanting to lean against the unsupported paper wall behind him, and rested his right elbow in his hand. A fitting song, given the box.

"Send for the others," Juliet said to the policeman. "We'll haul him to London."

CHAPTER 21

THE DARKNESS SHIFTED.

A haze of voices like water coursed somewhere in the shadows, and she flowed with them, bobbing up and down. Heavy enough that she feared she would sink.

She shifted again, and the voices grew louder, or perhaps she only heard more of them. Voices churning like a distant storm.

She jerked, and for a moment she felt weightless. Then her body hit something solid.

Somewhere in the black waters a thousand leeches burrowed into her skin, feasting and squirming, the pain lancing her skin.

She gasped.

"Get him *now!*" yelled a man's voice. "He doesn't need blood, she's covered in it!"

Something cold and metallic touched Ceony's skin and snaked up the length of her torso. A chill swept over her.

"He's here!" called a woman.

Somewhere in the shadows Ceony heard a man chanting, the

mumbling of old and unfamiliar words. She felt heat in her skin. She *knew* that heat.

The chanting paused. "Get the glass out, or the spell will do nothing," said the voice, calmer than the rest.

A wave struck Ceony, spinning her in the darkness. Rolling her over. A leech dropped from her skin, then another. The chanting resumed, as did the heat. Heat she had felt on Foulness Island.

Blurs of light mingled with the shadow. A broken sunrise.

An Excisioner.

No! Ceony's mind screamed, but her lips didn't move; her eyes didn't open.

The leeches fell away, burned away, and the water sucked her down until the voices faded.

When Ceony opened her eyes, a halo of electric bulbs, none of which were lit, stared down at her like glass eyes with filament pupils. She blinked, focusing her vision. The bulbs protruded out of swirls of brass, which joined together like an upside-down bouquet plugged into the gray-slab ceiling—a ceiling she didn't recognize.

She blinked again, slowly, her eyelids heavy. Her whole body felt heavy, as if it had been carved out of wood. Her dry tongue shifted in her dry mouth, tasting sand and sour. Her head ached— a calm, dull pounding deep in her brain.

She glanced down at an olive-colored blanket pulled up to her breasts, her arms lying parallel on top of it. A string with a tag hung off her left wrist. She stared at it until her eyes focused enough to read her name: Twill, Ceony. She shifted, feeling a stiff foreign material around her body. She craned against the thick pillow beneath her head to see what she was wearing—a white linen dress, or perhaps robe, that covered her nearly to the chin.

She looked to her right, taking in a row of empty hospital beds, white and flat with short, crib-like grating on the sides. An English flag and pole rested in the corner, near a door. A hospital. She was in a hospital.

When she looked to her left, a mobile curtain blocked her view of the rest of the large community room. Beside her bed rested a simple wooden chair without a cushion. The book *A Tale of Two Cities* lay open and upside down on it, about half-read.

She lifted her arm, surprised at its weight, and rubbed her eyes. She pulled it back and examined her hand.

That was when she remembered.

The house. Grath. The window, the mirrors. Blood, glass. Mg. Aviosky. Delilah.

She gripped the sides of the narrow mattress and tried to sit up, but the hospital spun around her and her empty stomach threatened to heave. She collapsed back onto the bed, the metal bars of its frame squeaking.

Once again, she lifted her hand and studied it, remembering the bits of glass that had been embedded in her flesh, remembering the pattern of the cuts marring her skin. She could still see them perfectly in her mind's eye, but her hand bore no bandages, no scars. She lifted her other one, remembering how the glass shard had cut into her fingers when she wielded it, but it was equally unscathed.

A dream? But it had been so vivid, so real. And why would she be in the hospital?

How was she even alive?

She prodded the back of her neck—her hair bound in a loose tail—and felt for bruises, scars, but the skin felt smooth to her touch. She pressed against her bruised cheek, but felt no pain, only the pressure of her own fingertips.

"Ceony."

She looked up to see Emery stepping around the curtain, dressed in the same clothes he had worn into the train station. Her heart raced at the sight of him, then drooped as she noticed the sling over his shoulder, cradling his right arm.

"You're hurt," she said, but the words came out as rasps.

Emery disappeared around the curtain, and she heard him call for water. Moments later a nurse in white came around the curtain with a pitcher and glass, which she set on a small table by Ceony's bed. She filled the glass partway, then helped Ceony lift her head so she could drink.

The water sent cold chills down her throat and into her arms and legs, but she swallowed it in one gulp. The nurse prepared a little more, urging her to drink in smaller sips.

Ceony finished and coughed. The nurse pressed a hand to her forehead. "You seem well," she said, "but I'll have the doctor look at you. How are you feeling?"

Ceony glanced from the nurse to Emery. "Feeling?" she repeated.

"Please," Emery said, "she only just awoke. Let me talk to her for a moment."

The nurse nodded and left, leaving the pitcher and cup behind.

Emery refilled the cup and sat on the chair, moving the novel to the floor. He took Ceony's hand in his—the one not held to his chest by the sling. His warm skin tickled hers.

Ceony pushed herself slightly more upright, though far from sitting. "Your arm," she said. "But you're safe."

He smiled at her, a genuine smile that lit up his eyes and carefully touched his lips. "My collarbone, actually," he said, "but seven more weeks should see it fine."

"Seven?" she repeated. She winced at a sharp pain in her head.

Emery squeezed her hand. "Do you hurt?"

"It's fine, I . . . How long have I been here?"

"Magician Hughes brought you here nine days ago," Emery said. "I've only been here for two."

"*Nine?*" Ceony repeated.

Emery nodded. "The spells they used on you are very draining on the body. They wanted you to wake on your own."

Ceony's breath quickened, and she felt panic forming in her belly. She remembered *something*, but the harder she tried to grasp it, the more it slipped away like river silt in her fingers.

Emery leaned forward and smoothed her hair. "Shhh, you're safe. You're well; we both are. You should rest."

"I've rested for nine days!" she exclaimed, but she paused and took a deep, deliberate breath, trying to settle herself. "What spells?"

Emery frowned. "The Cabinet does not like to advertise it, but not all Excision is illegal. A few are employed by them for cases such as yours."

Ceony's skin went cold. "An Excisioner . . . did something to me?" *Who did he kill in order to heal me?* Images of Delilah bound to her chair filled Ceony's mind.

Her skin rose in gooseflesh. Her intestines stirred.

"He healed you, yes," Emery said, and his frown turned to a flat line. His eyes were not impenetrable this time; they were filled with concern. "I wasn't here, I'm sorry. I left to protect you, but it seems that it was the last thing I should have done."

Ceony shook her head, her skull throbbing at the action. "Delilah, Aviosky. Grath—"

He ran his thumb over the back of her hand. "Grath is dead, and has already been cremated. Delilah . . ."

Ceony's mouth grew dry once more. "She's . . . she's okay?"

Emery lowered his eyes. "I'm sorry, Ceony."

Ceony bit the inside of her lip, but that didn't stop the tears from betraying her. Emery brought her knuckles—her unscathed knuckles—to his lips, but he didn't speak. Ceony pressed the sleeve of her other hand to her mouth to stifle a sob, and she sunk back into her pillow, staring at the ceiling, trying not to replay Delilah's murder in her head.

It reminded Ceony of Anise Hatter, her best friend from secondary school, who had killed herself. If Ceony had only gotten to her in time, she'd still be alive. Only this was even more Ceony's fault. Ceony *had* been there, and still . . .

The doctor arrived, and Emery stepped back as he listened to Ceony's heart, not commenting on her tears. He asked her questions in a paternal tone—how she felt, did her head hurt, did she have any pain—which Ceony answered with only nods. The doctor said she could check out in an hour and left, pulling the curtain closed for privacy.

Emery resumed his seat. They remained quiet for a long time.

After Ceony's tears dried to her cheeks, she asked, "Magician Aviosky?"

"Is alive and well, thanks to you," Emery said. "She's checked in twice a day since I arrived to see how you're faring."

Ceony took a deep breath, letting herself feel grateful that at least she'd managed to save one of them. "My family?"

"They're back home, preparing for a permanent move. Your parents were here this morning. You should call them after you're released." He paused. "I can call them, if you prefer."

"They're safe?" she asked, studying his eyes for their secrets. "Saraj?"

"Saraj has been incarcerated," Emery said, a finality to his words. His eyes hardened. "It was a matter of luck and trickery that got him there, but we managed it."

"We," she repeated. "You weren't alone."

"No. The Cabinet would never send a single man after an Excisioner." He glanced down to his sling.

"He's been jailed before, though."

Emery frowned. "Yes."

"And escaped."

"Not this time," he assured her. He sighed. "I'll tell you the rest later, when things have settled."

"Promise?"

"Promise."

Ceony stared at the ceiling for a long time, until Emery's chair scooted back and he stood.

"I'll contact your parents and finish your paperwork," he said.

Ceony squeezed his hand, halting him. "I have to tell you something," she whispered.

His brow rose, but he returned to his seat without question.

Ceony rolled her lips together and glanced around to ensure no one had snuck up on her. "He did it, Emery. He broke his bond with glass. Grath died an Excisioner. He . . . he bonded to Delilah's blood."

Emery frowned. "I feared as much, judging by the autop—by the information I received."

"But I broke my bond, too," she whispered. "I'm a Gaffer, Emery."

He leaned away from her, incredulous. "You sustained serious injuries, Ceony. You may be suffering—"

"Give me a mirror," she said. "I can prove it."

Emery held her gaze for a long moment, but finally stood from his chair and left. He returned a minute later with a small mirror on the end of a metal shaft, similar to the tool Ceony's dentist used to see the backs of her teeth.

Ceony took it from him. Touching the edges of the tiny mirror the way she had seen Delilah do it, she said, "Reflect."

She handed it back to Emery, whose eyes narrowed as he looked at the new image in the mirror. A picture of Delilah—her smiling face as it had looked the day Ceony dined with her at the bistro. The moment before their world had flipped over, leaving Ceony hanging by her fingernails and Delilah swimming in the dark.

Emery set the mirror down. "How?" he asked. "But perhaps I don't want to know."

"You bond to what your material is made of," Ceony whispered. "I did it with the wooden floorboards in Magician Aviosky's mirror room. Next you bond to yourself, and then to the new material. It breaks the bond, Emery, and seals a new one. I think I could do it again. I hope so. I don't want to be a Gaffer. But I need sand."

"Sand," he repeated, thoughtful.

She rolled onto her shoulder, clasping Emery's arm. "Please don't tell anyone," she begged. "If it falls into the wrong hands . . . Oh, Emery, what would Excisioners do with such magic? They're powerful enough already."

She thought of Delilah slumped in her chair and pushed the image away. A sore lump formed in her throat.

"You should report it," Emery said, lowering into the chair, "but I won't force you. And I won't say a word."

Ceony let out a long breath. "Thank you."

Emery nodded. He pulled his arm from her grasp and entwined his fingers with hers.

"She saved me," Ceony murmured. "Delilah saved me. She taught me the spells, not knowing I would use them. If she hadn't, I would be dead. Magician Aviosky would be, too. Grath wanted her heart."

Grath. Ceony shivered.

"What will they do?" she asked.

Emery leaned toward her. "What do you mean?"

"I . . . I killed him, Emery," she whispered. "I stabbed him and shattered the glass. I killed Grath."

"Saving your life as well as the life of a prestigious magician,"

Emery said. He released her hand and caressed her cheek. "If anything, Ceony, you'll be congratulated."

Ceony's stomach turned. "I don't want to be congratulated."

"Then you won't be," he promised. "It's over today. We'll go back home, if that's what you want. If you can bond to paper again."

Ceony nodded. "I do. And I can. I'm sure it will work."

Emery stood and bent over her and smoothed hair from her forehead.

"I'll go take care of things. I'll be right back, and then we'll go home together," he said.

Ceony nodded, a small warmth filling her heart. She clung to it, cherishing it, as she watched Emery go. Emery, the paper magician. How she loved him.

Grunting, Ceony pushed herself into a sitting position and reached for the pitcher, but she stopped halfway, studying her outstretched hand. The hand that had gripped the glass that killed Grath Cobalt. The hand that had made her a Gaffer.

She brought it closer to her face, tracing a finger over her palm and knuckles where the scars should have been. She was a Gaffer now, but tonight she would be a Folder again.

And Ceony realized she held the secret Grath had labored years to discover, the secret no living magician knew existed: the secret to breaking and resealing bonds. She was a Folder—she would always be a Folder—but she could be a Gaffer, too. Or a Pyre, a Siper, a Polymaker. She could even be a Smelter.

Balling her hand into a fist, Ceony twisted in her bed and looked out the window behind her, out into the yard of the hospital and the street beyond, where the buggies were parked bumper to bumper, and the first orange leaf of fall flew on the air, caught up by a summer wind. Ceony knew it then.

Starting today, she could be anything she wanted to be.

ACKNOWLEDGMENTS

THERE ARE *SO MANY* people I'm grateful to for helping with the fruition of this story. First is my husband, Jordan, who reads everything I send to him and listens to me talk talk talk about this book and others constantly, without ever a peep of complaint. A big thank-you also to my dedicated readers—Juliana, Lauren, Laura, Hayley, Andrew, Lindsey, Whit, Alex, and Bekah—all of whom helped me make this story decent.

Of course, I can't forget Marlene, who boosted me over the publishing fence with this series. I want to cheer for Angela Polidoro, who is a fantastic line editor, kiss the 47North team for their hard work, and extend my thanks to my editors David Pomerico and Jason Kirk for making my words palatable.

And, as always, my hat's off to God, who gave me the brain that comes up with all my ideas.

ABOUT THE AUTHOR

Kyndall Elliott, 2013

BORN IN SALT LAKE City, Charlie N. Holmberg was raised a Trekkie alongside three sisters who also have boy names. In addition to writing fantasy novels, she is also a freelance editor. She graduated from BYU, plays the ukulele, owns too many pairs of glasses, and hopes to one day own a dog.